ON THE BRINK OF DEATH

The WHITE FAN came at Rockson spinning the now opened fan in front of him like a toreador's cape, creating a dizzying blur of white. And again the Doomsday Warrior felt the seemingly harmless implement slam into him. Shots hit his face and throat and stomach in an unending barrage of blows sending Rock reeling backward as if he had been struck by a cannon shell. He fell down, landing on his back, not even able to soften the blow with his arms. He could feel his consciousness going out like a fading lightbulb. He had never felt so awkward, so humiliated. He couldn't even touch the man. All his years of training, of fighting, meant nil against one of the last living Masters.

Rock tried to rise from a sitting position and found his body barely responding to his commands. Even flesh and muscle as toughened as Rockson's had its limits. He wasn't a superman—just a man—and a very mortal one at that.

THE SURVIVALIST SERIES
by Jerry Ahern

#5: THE WEB (1145, $2.50)
Blizzards rage around Rourke as he picks up the trail of his family and is forced to take shelter in a strangely quiet Tennessee valley town. But the quiet isn't going to last for long!

#6: THE SAVAGE HORDE (1243, $2.50)
Rourke's search gets sidetracked when he's forced to help a military unit locate a cache of eighty megaton warhead missiles hidden on the New West Coast—and accessible only by submarine!

#7: THE PROPHET (1339, $2.50)
As six nuclear missiles are poised to start the ultimate conflagration, Rourke's constant quest becomes a desperate mission to save both his family and all humanity from being blasted into extinction!

#8: THE END IS COMING (1374, $2.50)
Rourke must smash through Russian patrols and cut to the heart of a KGB plot that could spawn a lasting legacy of evil. And when the sky bursts into flames, consuming every living being on the planet, it will be the ultimate test for THE SURVIVALIST.

#9: EARTH FIRE (1405, $2.50)
Rourke, the only hope for breaking the Russians' brutal hold over America, and the Reds fear the same thing: the imminent combustion of the earth's atmosphere into global deadly flames!

#10: THE AWAKENING (1478, $2.50)
Rourke discovers that others have survived the explosion of the earth's atmosphere into flames—and must face humans who live to kill and kill to live, eating the flesh of their victims!

DOOMSDAY WARRIOR #6

BY RYDER STACY

ZEBRA BOOKS
KENSINGTON PUBLISHING CORP.

ZEBRA BOOKS

are published by

Kensington Publishing Corp.
475 Park Avenue South
New York, NY 10016

First printing: September 1985

Printed in the United States of America

Chapter One

A field of death. A field of blood and rotting flesh. Where once had grown brilliant flowers and lush trees now lay only broken human stems with blood-red flowers of torn arms and shattered skulls. Where once had been what men called beauty was now just ugliness and decay. Nature in her harmony creates life, color, motion—things reaching up toward perfection. It is left to the creation called man to create her antithesis—black stillness in which twisted, broken things sink down into the ground in pools of festering poison.

Forrester Valley, where just the day before the battle had raged between the Freefighting forces of Century City and an invading Russian-controlled Nazi army of nearly a quarter of a million men. (*See Book #5*). Every Freefighter had been prepared to die—and had fully expected to as their 10,000 man force was vastly outnumbered by the Nazi forces. Yet in the midst of the darkest hours—a miracle. The Glowers, the hideously ugly mutant race whose bodies glowed with a deadly blue flame and whose minds with their telepathic powers were capable of healing—or killing—had arrived just when all seemed lost. As the German troops and heavy equipment had surged across the valley floor bent on complete annihilation of the Freefighters, the Glowers' huge sandships had appeared out of nowhere and tore into the ranks of the Nazis. They had unleashed the totality of their mental death—creating terrifying hallucinations in the Germans' minds. Whatever they feared most they had suddenly seen before them—and in striking out in their blind terror—had decimated one another. The dirty work had been done by their own foul unconscious memories and evil deeds, as they were literally consumed by their private nightmares. Within minutes the plains between the two low mountain ranges of the valley had been turned into an immense grave of bloody flesh and smoking white hot metal. Then the Glowers had disappeared as quickly as they had come, vanishing into the swirling clouds of mist at the far end of the Valley.

The Germans had pulled back in hysterical retreat—those who were still alive. Nearly 70% of their army had been destroyed—the supposedly invincible German military broken as easily as a twig. The Freefighting forces had stood up on their camouflaged mountain-top firing positions and cheered. Century City was saved and a blow had been struck for America's freedom that would ring throughout the land. They had quickly pulled back, wanting to vanish into the Colorado Rockies before reconnaissance planes could track them back to the hidden subterranean Century City. But many brave fighters had died that day and though victorious, the Freefighters limped back through the thick pine forests, carrying their wounded comrades-in-arms.

Even in victory one can suffer devastating losses. Nearly half of their fighting men had been killed. Century City itself had been nearly destroyed by a neutron bomb that had landed on Ice Mountain, the peak just to the north of Century City's own Carson Mountain—beneath which C.C. had been built. And though none of them yet knew it, perhaps the greatest catastrophe of all—for as Ted Rockson and Rona Wallender stood looking at the destruction, one of a final volley of tank shells from the retreating Germans went off right next to them, blasting both into the air. They lay side by side, badly hurt, unconscious in the midst of the plateau filled with the dead and dying bodies of German and American fighters. Death walked in his dark robes that night, searching among the fallen warriors for those who were ready to be taken down into his dark domain.

But even death, which takes the souls of things, leaves behind their lifeless, discarded shells. The forces of nature move in quickly to devour the putrid refuse, to turn it back into the stuff of life. As the bodies slowly cooled, as their hearts stopped and their brains which had once thought and loved, turned into a rotting mush, nature's first line of scavengers—microbes and bacteria rushed in to eat their fill. They dug into the hardening flesh with microscopic shovel-like teeth, ripping out infinitesimal bites again and again. Then came the larger flesh-eaters—flies and wasps taking their due, depositing their eggs inside the corpses so that their own young might hatch and eat their way out into a forbidding world. Then the wolves and wild dogs appeared, furtively edging closer, circling the dead with wild red eyes until they were sure that no danger was present, no men with their sticks that spoke loud death.

Then they lunged forward with desperate hunger, their fanged jaws ripping out whole chunks of flesh, dismembering the dead Nazis and Americans as they chewed away fiercely on their joints—knees, shoulders, ankles, then running off with their bloody dinners, trailing veins and chunks of human meat. Within 18 hours of the battle for Forrester Valley that had been responsible for this vast graveyard, every corpse was being attacked, mutilated, eaten.

At last the human predators arrived. Dark men with equally dark robes that fell to their ankles, rushing among the fallen fighters, searching for any that still lived, any that would fill their needs—Slave Traders—peddlers in human flesh. Flesh that still functioned, flesh that could be sold to live out their wretched lives in factories and work gangs. And here and there among the cold dead they found what they sought—men, bloodied, grievously wounded—but still among the world of the living. They smashed at the groaning, fallen fighters rudely awakening them from their dark dreams into an even darker reality, hitting them with clubs, kicking them with steel-tipped boots, until they were forced against their own will into consciousness. The Slave Traders rushed over the three mile-wide plateau that looked down over the center of the Valley where the largest battle of the post-nuke world had just taken place and gathered their crops. What the grim reaper had sowed with a bloody scythe, they now gathered. The fruits of destruction.

Something was smashing him in the face. The blows jarring him like the screaming gong of an immense brass bell, shaking his skull so violently he could feel his brain slamming up against the curved bone. He tried to raise his arms which felt leaden and dead to protect himself, but this only increased the force of the blows against his temple and cheek and mouth. His eyes one violet, one aquamarine, opened the blinding light of the sun ripping into them like razor blades, slicing his pupils, making him cry out in pain. He tried to roll to the side to avoid the continuing barrage of blows as his eyes quickly adjusted to the burning white bulb of the sun hovering over the trees that dotted the near mountains. Suddenly the flaming orb was blotted out by a dark angular-faced man, wearing a long black robe. The man kicked out again with his long leg.

"Up, up vomitous cur," the attacker screamed down from high above in heavily foreign-accented English. A gnarled cane came soaring down attached to the end of the dark man's hand and hit the wounded man on the shoulder, sending waves of sharp pain through it. The man on the ground tried to gather himself but everything was just a swirling dream of pain and incomprehension.

Where was he? Who was he? He felt as if he had been falling down an endless pit so black that nothing could be seen. Nothing. And now . . . Now he must survive. Whatever was happening to him, the instinctive urge to survive was supreme. He rose to one knee and then shakily stood up as his attacker let fly with one more furious smash with the oak cane darkened with a thousand coatings of blood to a dark, violent purple.

"Over there," the voice above screamed out shrilly, pointing to the right with the tip of the 7.2mm Turgenev service revolver he held in his other hand. The aching, wounded man looked over, his eyesight at last coming into a clear focus. Lines of men, their torn and bleeding bodies covered with tattered Freefighter uniforms oozing with swatches of bright red, were being herded along by others of the dark stubble-faced men, each garbed in the same dark robes as his attacker. The man looked around as he stood to his full height; every nerve, every cell in his body aching as if they were on fire. There had obviously been a battle of some sort here—and recently. Stiff corpses dotted the crater-pocked ground, their skin pale as the moon, their eyes and tongues already eaten away by lines of large red ants. The wounded man looked down as he nearly stumbled. He was standing in a black-charred blast crater himself. He must have been lying there when the first blows hit. But before—what was before? He searched frantically in his mind for anything, anything that would tell him *who* he was.

The attacker, holding the pistol at his side walked ahead a few yards and kicked at one of the bodies which rolled to the side, its rock hard arms stretched straight out in front as if it were reaching for something.

"Damn—almost all these fucking things are dead," the robed man said, spitting out a gob of dark slime from between brown, cracked teeth. He kicked at another of the myriad bodies on the plateau and this time elicited a faint groan. The robed man bent over and looked at the wounded fighter lying prone on the bloody soil. But a quick glance at the missing right leg, torn off jaggedly at the knee, showed him that it was just a piece of garbage. Of no use to him, to anyone. He placed the muzzle of the pistol against the mortally wounded man's temple and pulled the trigger. The head erupted into a frenzy of spiraling red pulp and the moans ceased.

The robed man stood up and glanced furtively around as the angrily burning sun rose above the horizon and sent down its killing radiation through the atomically thinned atmosphere of the earth, an atmosphere ripped apart by the thousand nuclear blasts a century earlier. Its entire molecular harmony disrupted, it now allowed in far more gamma, x-rays, cosmic rays and every other goddamned ray one could name than the old earth could have imagined. The robed-one winced at its brightness and spun his head around, suddenly noticing the man he had just been kicking seconds before, standing, staring at him with wide uncomprehending eyes.

"Fool," the robed man said angrily, raising the blue nickelplated revolver until it was aimed directly at the man's chest. "Are you so eager to join your dead comrades here?" The wounded man looked down again at the dead and dying, at the endless stretches of arms and legs and bodyless heads. His comrades?

He didn't know them. Nor who they were, nor what war they had been fighting. Why couldn't he remember anything. He could think, he could understand words. He could instantly comprehend the world in all its darkness around him. But beyond that—he knew nothing. It was as if his life had begun at the moment the robed man had begun hitting at him. As if he had been born out of those blows. Out of . . . out of what . . .

His confusion was shattered by the sharp crack of the pistol and the bullet that dug out a little hole in the hard-packed dirt next to his foot.

"The next one goes in your chest, scum." The robed figure aimed the pistol right at him, dead on his heart, and closed one eye sighting down the dark barrel. The wounded man, not a seeker of his own death, turned and walked toward the group of about forty other wounded men surrounded by more robed flesh-takers. Ted Rockson, the Doomsday Warrior, his chest and arms covered with dried blood and a five-inch-long, deep gash across the side of his head, joined the prisoners being gathered by the gang of Slavers. The tank shell blast that had nearly killed him and Rona, cracking his skull like an earthquake fissure had done more than just rip his flesh—it had created a total amnesia in the still reeling brain tissue. His entire life history had been taken from him, sent into the dark recesses of his unconscious where the memory patterns lay dormant, hidden from his mental reach.

The fiery blast that had exploded just feet from the two Freefighters had singed the top of Rockson's scalp down to the flesh, leaving only blackened hair stubs—and the hurricane of dirt that had knocked them both to the ground had flown into his eyes, leaving them puffed and bloodshot, the lids all swollen and red. Thus, even his own men who glanced at him as he joined in their ranks didn't recognize him—his white streak of hair now blackened, his mismatched violet and aquamarine eyes, hardly visible beneath the grotesquely distended eyelids. He was just another lost soul, hurt and in shock, unfortunate enough to have been left behind as the Freefighting army retreated back to Century City to gather their strength and treat the wounded.

One of the Slavers pushed him brusquely into the crowd as he sauntered over. Rockson looked frantically around at the downcast prisoners, trying to remember, trying to recognize even a single face. If he had been with these men, had fought alongside them—perhaps they would know him, could tell him who he was, what had happened. He turned toward one of them, a large blond-haired fellow who didn't seem too badly hurt other than a long gash along his right arm which he had covered with his shirt.

"I—I—", Rockson didn't even know how to phrase the question. "I seem to have lost my memory, mister," The Doomsday Warrior said haltingly. "Do you know me?" The blond man looked him up and down, then stared long and hard into his swollen, purple bruised face. He shook his head slowly as he stepped back.

"Can't say that I do," the man said. "But you must be from Century City. A Freefighter—those are the only people—the only Americans who would be lying around here. Although I did hear that detachments from some of the other Free Cities had come to our aid. So I suppose it's possible you're from one of them. Although, to be perfectly honest, mister, you look a mess. I don't know if your own mother would recognize you right now."

"Century City? Freefighter?" Rockson asked almost in a whisper. "The words sound so familiar, yet—I can't—"

"Yeah, you took a bad wound there," the blond Freefighter said, pointing at the side of Rock's head. "You can't remember nothing, huh?" He looked at Rockson again, trying to see beneath the blood-coated face, trying to place him. "I just don't know you, man—though there is something vaguely familiar." He looked at Rock with pity and then trying to reassure him said, "Don't worry about it, mister. From what I read once about amnesia—it usually disappears once the shock to the brain wears off. You'll remember in time—though I don't know how much good it will do you—we're prisoners of the Reds now. Not the Regular Army—these guys are Slavers. The Russians let them take the remains of their battles. We'll probably be sold off to some Fortress City to work out our lives in some godforsaken sweathole of a factory making underwear for Russian officers." The blond man smiled grimly, a sardonic look of ultimate resignation crossing his broad face.

"It's kind of ironic," he went on, softly. "We, that is, Century City won—and yet those of us here—lost. I guess we just have to think of ourselves as sacrifices for the greater good. Shit—if I'd just woken up a few minutes earlier. Took a bad shot myself," he said, showing Rockson a swollen deep wound on his upper chest. "Anyway—name's Swenson, Craig Swenson—glad to meet you." He held out a meaty hand which Rockson took, happy for the momentary human friendship in the midst of the death and stench of the charnel grounds around them.

"Wish I could tell you mine but—"

"It don't matter much, anyway," Swenson went on. "You won't be needing your old name soon. Once we're put into work gangs in the factories or out in the radioactive rubble, clearing off land for their agricultural stations—they'll give us new names—slave names."

The Slavers, in their filthy dark robes that swirled around them, concealing countless pistols, daggers and other devices of dealing pain and death, continued racing around the battlefield that had once been Forrester Valley—before the battle that had killed upward of 300,000 men in less than five hours. It was the largest number of soldiers killed in such a short time in any battle in the history of human warfare. But no one was around to record such statistics anymore. Survival in post-nuke war America was its own reward. Most of the fallen troops were just dead, half devoured meat around the mountain tops, slopes and the valley floor itself. But here and there among the carnage the human scavengers did manage to rouse a few dozen more souls.

The moaning and tattered crowd of America survivors grew to nearly 80 men, surrounded by dozens of the Slavers who took chains out of a beat-up old Red Army supply truck and attached them to the prisoners' feet and hands. Several resisted—but they were slammed to the ground with rifle butts and locked up along with the rest. Rockson himself felt the deep urge to fight back—but it was suicide to try anything. He felt as if he were in the middle of a nightmare where nothing is known, and death is everywhere.

Who am I? Who the fuck am I? But his probing thoughts met only a wall as hard as granite beyond which was only swirling blackness. He was without a single recollection of his past life.

At last the Slavers had gathered all that was worth taking from the death fields and herded the prisoners out, heading down an ancient dirt road toward the north. The captured Americans walked in single file, chained to the man in front of them. Many of the more seriously wounded were barely able to walk—the clanking chains around their ankles only adding to the weight they must drag. But they all knew that to fall meant death—instantaneously. The Slavers screamed out curses at them to move faster, to stay in line, frequently slashing out with long leather whips at any recalcitrant prisoners. They headed off down the winding dusty dirt road, created nearly two hundred years before by cows and horse drawn wagons. A time when America had belonged to Americans. Their eyes rested heavily on the ground, their heads unable to rise, to look at the mountains that lay ahead, to look toward a destiny that none of them wished to contemplate.

Chapter Two

Hours before Rockson was kicked into consciousness and imprisoned, Rona had waked from her blast-induced sleep and staggered to her feet. Her combat outfit was ripped and shredded by the tank shell. It had been light—now the moon was low in the sky. She had been out for hours, many hours. Her body felt like death warmed over, as every muscle protested any motion in throbbing stabs of pain. Rock? She suddenly remembered—he had been there with her.

She turned around with such force that her skull and neck lit up with a literally blinding pain, almost knocking her out. But she didn't care about pain—just Rockson. She lowered herself to one knee and looked at the badly wounded man who lay there bathed in the cold rays of the moon, still and ghostly looking. She lowered her head to his chest and listened—the heartbeat felt strong. She knew his strength, his deep physical resources—either something would have to kill him outright or he would live through it. But he was obviously hurt, breathing slowly and deeply, mouth open in complete unconscious relaxation. She tried to reach out with her mind, as he had taught her to do. Again, the screaming pain went through her head, but she continued. To no avail. Either she wasn't sending properly or he just couldn't receive. She had to get help and fast. She would never let him die.

Rona rose to her feet, again almost losing her balance as every movement seemed to go right through her central nervous system. All around her was the devastation of the Battle of Forrester Valley—big holes gouged out of the living soil, bodies and parts of bodies strewn wildly around, trees leveled into mounds of toothpicks. She walked over to the edge of the plateau from which the Freefighters had been firing on the Nazi forces and looked down. The moon's vibrant blue rays illuminated the vast carnage below—burning tanks and half-tracks, craters a 10-ton truck could drive through, and bodies, endless piles of corpses. It was hard to believe that so many people existed, let alone that so many had died.

Suddenly she saw a flash of light, then several, glinting along far below through the graveyard. It could be Freefighters, Rona thought, straining to see—or it could be Reds. She glanced over at Rockson, just yards away, who lay as still and calm as a statue, bathed in the faint light of the moon. She'd have to take a chance. She scoured around and found a coil of rope in a dead Nazi's backpack, and headed over the edge down the steep mountain slope. The valley floor was nearly 1,000 feet down through loose gravel and treacherous footholds, but by using the rope as a guide Rona moved like a mountain goat, having trained in rapelling and other rope climbing techniques.

She had barely reached the death-strewn valley floor and started toward the moving figures some half mile off when she heard a familiar thudding sound—a Red chopper—and it was heading right toward her, its huge searchlight mounted underneath scanning the ground searching for something. And from the other flank, coughing vehicles suddenly lumbered forth—five flatbed trucks with a hodge-podge of different-sized tires beneath them, and various rusting machineguns nailed down to their flat carriages. Riding in the cabs and on the back were fierce-looking men with bald heads, gold earrings, immense mustaches and beards, and long curved swords dangling from their sides. She knew what they were—Slavers—human slime who preyed on the wounded.

She looked around for a place to hide and dove into a 100mm mortar-created hole nearby. But voices instantly rang out over a loudspeaker from the helicopter which stopped and hovered above her, aiming the blinding light down.

"She's there—right below us. A young one—looks like a mutant." The chopper, which Rona could now see wasn't a Red chopper but an old U.S. Army helio, outfitted with all kinds of half-falling off armaments, kept the tower of light on her while the scar-covered and tattooed Slavers jumped down from the trucks and surrounded her. Inside the 15-foot wide, six-foot high crater Rona grabbed a knife from the outstretched hand of a Nazi corpse and turned slowly around, ready for all comers.

"Careful," a voice yelled out. "A goodlooking healthy mutant woman would be worth her weight in gold."

"Yes, better if she has all her limbs," another growling half-human voice screamed out. "Don't rip her." They came down the crater edge from all sides moving slowly, their hands outstretched to grab her. One of them, a big one, with practically no face at all, leaped at her—and got a 14" bayonet blade through his kidney, pancreas and various other organs. He tumbled to her feet as Rona whipped the blade out, wiped it twice on her already blood-soaked khaki trousers and held it up again, the moon bouncing slivers of crystal light off the razor-sharp knife.

"Next," she said, motioning for them to come forward with her other hand. Four of them leaped at once, screaming and spitting to frighten her. She lashed out twice and the blade ripped two thick bellies. But something was hitting her from behind. Again—she fell back into the darkness from which she had only minutes before awakened.

Rona woke up staring up at the brilliant blue sky laced with spider webs of purple from the back of a speeding flatbed truck. She was tied hand and foot, tightly. And she was naked. Evidently they had carefully inspected the merchandise.

"Red hair good," a voice suddenly snarled down as one of the Slavers came up behind her. "Here, water, water. Don't dry up. You are beauty—yes? Too bad you so good—or I would have you. But you are worth much—very much. You have good teeth. Here, we rub cactus salve on your wounds." He smiled a toothless grin and squeezed her bare left breast, then slopped a blue paste on he and began rubbing it over her chest, nearly salivating as he did so. She had the sudden urge to shout out, "No, no, my name is Rona Wallender, Freefighter," but bit her lip. They didn't know who she was. If they did, they would sell her to the Reds or the Nazis for sure. She'd be tortured, or worse. Used to lure Rockson and other Freefighters to her. She would say nothing. Just another slave. There would be no special interest in her beyond her beauty. She would be sold to some fat rich slug from whom it would be possible to escape.

"Where are we going," she asked the slobbering ugly creature touching the whole front of her body now, his foul breath making her nauseous.

"We going to Goerringrad, new Nazi Fortress City near here. Got 'emselves a slave market there. Gonna fetch a pretty price for you. Red hair, nice long legs, pretty nose—glad your face no got cut. Too bad I poor man," he smiled with all the toothless charm he could muster, "otherwise *I* buy you."

Suddenly she felt woozy, her head spinning into that kaleidoscopic darkness that she had seen so much of of late.

"Good, happy juice hit you now. Now you be friendly to men you meet—no more hellcat. You be easy, and smile. That be good for sale. When drug wear off—they realize you tiger." He laughed out loud, this apparently being a quite humorous idea to a Slaver. "But too late—we got rubles! You go sleep now." He patted her head, getting dirt on it. "Long trip. Want you to look pretty. When you wake we dress you in harem clothes—lots of silk, thin material, see-through, pretty. You be real nice for auction tomorrow."

She tried to fight off the drug they had put in her water, but found everything revolving around her at a faster and faster speed. No, she didn't want to go under again. It was frightening, horrible. She fought with all her strength, but to no avail. Her mind slowly but inevitably sank beneath the waves of perception and into a drugged dreamland.

Chapter Three

There have been many "Long Marches" in history—Mao's march to Peking during the Communist takeover, the Japanese Death March for American prisoners on Bataan, the Cambodian march of all the inhabitants of the Asian nation's cities, by the Khmer Rouge guerrillas, into the countryside to implement their "agrarian policies" in which nearly half the country's six million people died. The annals of human cruelty are filled with marches of death in which the victor's bullets don't even have to be wasted on their prisoners. The captured soldiers or civilian populations kill themselves by the sheer effort of forcing their wounded and tired bodies to go on mile after torturous mile. For to stop is instant death—and any man would prefer the chances of survival, however slim, to the barrel of a gun pointing in his eyes and the shrill scream of the slug that will take his life.

The Slavers took Rockson and the 80 or so other men they had gathered, on *their* version of the Death

March. The women and younger boys that their other unit had captured had already been taken to the slave market in Goerringrad where they would be sold to the highest bidder—men who would use them for their own "pleasures" until the young beauties were used up. Then they would be discarded like so much garbage—sold into whorehouses or into the back-breaking labor camps where life was measured in months rather than years.

The group of men which Rockson was in was already consigned to the S.S. of Goerringrad. The S.S. Col. Struhl, Quartermaster of the Fortress City, had told Yigmar, the leader of this particular band of Slavers, that they would pay cold cash—gold rubles—on delivery for able-bodied men who could be used to build roads, landing fields, housing. "But don't bring us any garbage," Struhl had warned him, "or you will take their place." Thus Yigmar, riding in a rusting 40-year old Red Army jeep with a black flag of chains around a skull snapping in the wind on the front right bumper, had decided on the Death March as a way to weed out the undesirables. Those who made it were obviously strong enough to work for the Nazis, those that didn't—well. The weaker died all the time, every second, everywhere on earth.

"Water, water," an aging Freefighter walking along the dusty road a few feet away from Rockson cried out for the fifth time in the last minute. His lips were dry as sand, with a thick white foam surrounding his mouth. His eyes kept rolling up in his head as he stumbled along. Rock kept leaning over to lend a supporting hand but a guard would rush over and slam at his arm with the butt of his Kalashnikov, screaming, "No help. Must walk on own." It was a game of ultimate stakes and every player was on his own.

Rockson was near the very back of the file of bedraggled, captured Americans. All of them were Freefighters from Century City and a few of the other nearby Freefighting cities who had lent support. All of them somehow left behind, unconscious, wounded, hidden beneath other bodies. They were brothers in war and wanted nothing more than to aid their weakening comrades faltering on the long march. For some men it is easier to die oneself than to see one's friends, fellow warriors through countless battles, dying alongside, and be able to do nothing. Every hour or so one of the men, their wounds just too severe, would collapse, falling over on the dusty back road, like a tree whose roots have been cut. Even the slamming of the Slaver's steel-tipped boots into their ribs wouldn't make them move. So they were left, without water or shade, to die in the roasting sun, baked red and literally cooked to death before this day came to an end. Within 12 hours of the start of the Death March ten of the prisoners lay along the sides of the road, their lives slipping away like so much dust in the wind. And there was still nearly 50 miles to go before reaching Goerringrad.

Rockson was sickened by the sight of the wounded being left like worthless beasts. He felt a fury inside of him that threatened to explode out at any moment. He didn't know who he was but he knew *what* he was—a fighter. His powerful arms, his heightened senses, the almost endless energy that his body seemed to possess, carrying him along the road with almost no effort. Even the lack of water didn't bother him. Somehow, he was different from the rest. There were many things about him which seemed strange. He could almost hear—not the words—but somehow the thoughts of the men around him, the prisoners and the guards. It seemed to happen when he was looking at a tree or the sky for a second and forgot where he was. His body relaxed—then it would occur, the world would start broadcasting out its thoughts, emotions, from all around him. The energy felt like an attack to him and he would tense up in fighting readiness—instantly the signals would vanish. But it was strange. He knew that men did not possess telepathy—yet he did. But when he reached deeper inside for his identity it was like coming up against a brick wall, a steel wall, completely impenetrable.

The Slavers marched them until midnight and Yigmar pulled the convoy of human commerce over to the side of the road.

"We rest scum. Give them water—but no food," he ordered his dozen or so heavily armed guards who surrounded them. He would cull out the weak, but it was madness to let them all die, they had to at least be given water. Tomorrow those who still lived when they reached Goerringrad would be given huge meals, fattened up, before presentation to the S.S. Quartermaster. And then Yigmar would get the gold. Ah, what a satchel of rubles this crew would bring in.

His guards went slowly down the rows of captured Freefighters doling out one cup of the precious fluid to each man. They drank it down in a second, many of them spilling half the contents in their mad desire for water, water to wet their parched throats. Then they fell into deep dark sleeps filled with nightmares.

Rockson watched it all with a bitter taste in his mouth. He leaned back against a tree, his eyes like twin radar domes absorbing everything in sight. The men around him were already asleep, breathing in harsh raspy tones. But Rockson couldn't sleep. His mind was awash with thoughts, half perceived images. It was as if the other part of him—the part that had somehow been put into the deep freeze—was trying to make contact with him. It was like hearing voices calling out from the far side of the moon, indistinct, like leaves whispering in the wind. Somehow the combined energies of not knowing who the hell he was plus being a prisoner of these Slavers and seeing the men dying all around him—all pushed him to the point of what felt like madness. He wanted to explode, to grab one of the guards and destroy him with a smash to the throat. He knew how to kill, just the thought of attacking brought up myriad ways to disable, punches, kicks, throws, that he hadn't even known he knew. But then what? He would get one, two, three . . . and then they would start firing blindly and all these men around him would be dead. He would have to wait, bide his time. And somehow he would have to find out who he was before he exploded in a rage of volcanic fury.

The next morning the slaves were awakened early just as the pale sun hobbled limply into the bruised purple sky, as if it had been fighting its own battles during the night. The Slavers rushed around the sleeping prisoners and kicked and cracked them with gunbutts and boots forcing them to rise to a standing position. Yigmar's tent was being stowed in the second jeep. When he was ready the Death march started again. And this time the prisoners felt even more agony than yesterday. Their muscles were tight as steel cords from the endless walking. Their chests and necks felt as if they were filled with burning needles.

But they knew that they would live or die by what happened today. And every man reached down into the center of his soul for the strength to get through it. They started along the dirt, single-lane road, heading north. Around them the terrain seemed to be getting richer, more bushes, thick green-leafed trees, lending from time to time their precious shade from the blistering sun. Occasionally a rabbit or absurdly groping groundhog would rush away from the road and into the surrounding dense vegetation as the prisoners came marching up. The men looked at the vanishing meat with wide eyes for not one of them had eaten now for nearly three days. They would have devoured the small mammals raw at that moment, ripping them apart, splattering their faces with hot blood. Their stomachs felt hollow as balloons while the acids of their own digestive systems were eating away at the lining, sending ripples of sharp pain through their guts.

Suddenly it was all too much for one man. He rushed toward a disappearing cottontail, his hands outstretched in mindless hunger, his brain forgetting where he was. Six rifles barked out and six burning slugs ripped into his back, sending him flying forward, his dead face smashing into a rock sending his teeth flying out in a spray of white pebbles.

The other Freefighters and Rockson, surged forward, but the rifles barked out again and two more Americans fell down in the dirt.

"Stop, stop," Yigmar screamed, standing on the front seat of his jeep some 75 feet ahead. He raised his long curved scimitar, striking as fierce a pose as possible. The golden rubles were slipping from his fingers with every lifeless body that crashed to the ground.

"Come, come," Yigmar said, grinning a gold-toothed smile at the inflamed prisoners. "Now is not the time to rebel. If you wanted to fight us, you should have done so on the battlefield. Trip almost over for you now. Just a few more hours—you get food, get places to live, work to do. Not so bad. Many have much worse." He smiled idiotically at them trying to make it all sound like some sort of idyllic paradise. Not one believed him, but the few seconds of time of his words bought cooled their tempers from the explosive to the boiling point. They settled back into their ranks, their heads bowed in shame and repressed rage as they walked along, their ankle chains clanking loudly.

They marched through the day, until the sun at last began setting again, falling from the purple blue sky like a silver gull hunting for darting fish just below the horizon. Those of the prisoners who were going to, had died already. The rest seemed to be surviving, Yigmar noted with satisfaction. He had only lost 10 of the original 80—better than usual.

"We almost there," he screamed out. "Just hour or two—then food." He smiled again, though not a man could see the artificially stretched mouth in the semi-darkness. The stars filled the vast skies like a billion little lips all opening and closing, sucking in the waste of the universe. After a time the moon suddenly appeared over a grove of trees, illuminating the road with a merciless light. At last the low walls of the Fortress City of Goerringrad appeared ahead, just as they came over a rise in the road. They could see thousands of lights twinkling in the mild breeze, and could, even from several miles off, hear the sounds of heavy machinery, of engines roaring. The Nazis were working non-stop on building their American headquarters, work-crews going around the clock with giant floodbeams lighting their task.

In their hunger and weariness, the prisoners prayed that they would get to eat and have a night's sleep before they would be forced to whatever jobs they would have to work at. God knew what their fate would be, though everyone of them had in the back of his mind the surety that he would escape, once he had regained strength, once his wounds were healed. These were Freefighters, not groveling slaves of the work sectors of the Russian cities. If they could just survive the next few days, weeks, they would get the hell out of here and rejoin their comrades in the hidden cities. Only that thought kept them from ending their lives right then and there.

Chapter Four

They were marched up to the steel gates of Goerringrad where four machine gun emplacements were manned, their huge .55mm muzzles aimed at all four roads that met in front of the fortress entrance. Yigmar showed his papers to the bored officer on duty who walked over and looked the new slaves up and down, making sure they were properly secured, shaking their chains, checking the locks. He would pay if some should escape and cause any harm. But satisfied that they were all incapacitated, he waved the slave convoy through. The other soldiers laughed and pointed at the American prisoners.

"So these are the fierce American warriors," one said in broken German-English.

"Now I know why I was so afraid to come over here," another laughed. The Freefighters gritted their teeth. They knew this would be only the first of many insults they would endure during their captivity. Rockson's eyes met the eyes of the lieutenant in charge. The German felt the strangest sensation run up and down his spine as if he had looked into the eyes of death incarnate.

"Stop! Stop!" he yelled, rushing over to the Doomsday Warrior. "Who is this man?" he demanded of Yigmar.

"Just a worthless American piece of scum," the Slave Master answered apologetically. "For what reason does he even catch your attention?"

"There is something about him—those eyes." The officer walked around Rockson looking him up and down while the Freefighter stood motionless as a rattler ready to strike. The Nazi walked back around in front of Rockson and stared into his eyes from only inches away. He wanted the slave to back down, to avert his gaze from his superior. But Rock just looked back, his eyes as cold and unbending as the stars above, fearing nothing. At last it was the Nazi's eyes which broke as he felt his very will going under the gaze. He had the sudden urge to shoot the man where he stood. But he knew the S.S. needed every man they could get. There would be an investigation. Better to do nothing.

"On with you then," the officer said, smirking as he walked back to his own troops, acting cocky as if he had made the prisoner bend under him. "Just another piece of slime," he laughed to the heavily armed Germans he commanded. "Soon he will be in the swamps."

The human cargo marched through the wide gates of the fortress and into the recently built city. Though the Nazis had been here less than six months they had already constructed nearly a square mile of barracks, munitions dumps, officers' headquarters, a landing field and generating plant. But then the Nazis have always been a most efficient organization. Yigmar drove ahead of the column of slaves through the absolutely straight streets that had been planned with typical German logical perfectionism in mind—the entire expanding Fortress laid out in rigidly symmetrical lines on every side—a perfect square with a hundred little perfect squares within it.

Rock saw with disgust the American slave teams being herded around like so many cattle to their backbreaking jobs. These weren't Freefighters—there weren't many of them within the Fortress walls as most would die before being captured.

The slaves who tramped along the wide main central avenue of Goerringrad looked as if they were not long for this earth. The Germans fed them enough, but kept them going day after day, in 16 hour shifts, without a day of rest. It was more functional for them, they had calculated, to push the workers to their limits—let them die—and replace them with new ones. And with men like Yigmar out there doing their collection work for them it was all quite simple.

Yigmar's jeep pulled up in front of a large concrete building, one of the biggest in the fortress and stopped. He disappeared within its ominous walls and within minutes reemerged with a gaunt-faced S.S. major who walked quickly down the rows of prisoners observing each one carefully. His eyes seemed devoid of the slightest shred of humanity or compassion—just two floating icebergs in a frigid sea. He came to Rockson but the Doomsday Warrior looked down. No sense to challenge every one of these bastards. Just act the humble slave—until the strength could emerge. Maj. Krupt reached the last man and headed back toward Yigmar.

"Yes, yes, these will do. Your selections are getting better, my greedy friend," Krupt said with a razor-thin grin, the writhing white moon far above reflecting its cutting rays off his golden S.S. symbols with their skull emblem, so that they looked as if they were on fire, glowing, illuminated from below by the very burning darkness of the man's soul. The S.S. man snapped his fingers together and an orderly ran over with a large leather bag that looked quite heavy from the way he held it tightly to his chest.

"Here," Krupt said, as Yigmar grabbed the bag and opened the cord at the top. His eyes widened as if they would pop out of his skull and a lascivious smile crossed his thick lips as he ran his fingers through the shimmering gold coins within.

"We need more," Krupt said, slapping a pair of black gloves he held in one hand into the palm of the other. "Many more. You will now be paid even more. And for every group of slaves over 100 you can bring us—an extra thousand ruble bonus." Yigmar's eyes widened even more. He was the smartest man alive. Everything he did was right. Why, he would be a rich man, perhaps the richest in America in a year or two if this kept up. A fortune in the flesh trade. And one thing about people—there were always plenty more where these came from.

"I will do my best, Herr Commandant," Yigmar said, bowing low as if to an emperor.

"Yes, yes, I'm sure you will," Krupt smirked, understanding the deep greed that motivated the man. "Just make sure they're not Russian or German," Krupt added ominously. "Because should I ever find out that even one of our men has been hurt or captured by you . . . well, I think you understand. We will take them from here. Men—" Krupt ordered, as a phalanx of underlings surrounded the now 70 prisoners and led them off toward their barracks. The workers huts were at the northern edge of the camp, barely habitable concrete barracks with the walls already collapsing in many places, without glass in the window frames, or doors in the unfinished entrances. The Germans had more important things to do than add the finishing touches to slaves' houses. As they were led down the narrow street, lit by rows of high floodlights the new prisoners were split up, four or five at a time pushed brusquely into one of the barracks. Rockson being last in line ended up at the last of the cement hovels at the very northern perimeter that the camp had reached thus far. On the other side were rows of barbed wire and floodlights with machine gun emplacements every two hundred feet.

One of the Nazi guards pushed him forward into the darkness. Rockson felt himself hurtling forward but managed to curve his arms in a half circle so he landed with a roll—on top of something soft.

"You'll be unchained in the morning," the guard yelled out as he stomped off.

"What the fuck," a voice screamed out of the darkness below Rockson's arms where he had fallen. He sensed a blow coming up and pulled himself backward. Sure enough, a fist flew by where his head had been and in the semi-darkness, as his eyes adjusted a little he could see the narrow glinting of a blade. The Doomsday Warrior jumped to his feet and backed off a yard.

"Don't want no trouble whoever I just fell on," he said, trying to sound friendly. "The guard pushed me and—"

"Shut up you," a voice sneered from several yards ahead of him. Suddenly the 40×50 foot spartan concrete shell was lit by the single flame of a candle from the far side of the room. Rockson could see that the floor was filled with slaves all sleeping on coats or little piles of straw or just thin strips of cardboard—anything, to protect them from the frigid cold of the concrete. Nearly every square foot of the floor was taken, each man somehow just fitting in between the arms and legs of those around him, so the entire group was bunched together like some insane jigsaw puzzle of humanity. The commotion had awakened them from their dark driftings and they leaned up one elbow to watch the confrontation.

"Who you, man?" the body Rockson had landed on yelled out. By the flickering light of the single candle Rock could see that the man was huge and tough as nails. Probably the ruler of this little roost, Rock thought, as he took in with revulsion the primitive state of the inhabitants. Their hair was matted thick as dirty mops, their scalps having been untouched by water for as long as any could remember. Their flesh was filled with sores, many of them open and oozing thin trails of pus. Most of the slave laborers had half their teeth missing, inflamed white gums filled their mouths. Their clothes were torn and ripped apart as if they had been worn for years, and were so coated with dirt and mud and slime that all were the same dark blackish brown without a trace of their original color left. The barrack dwellers looked at Rockson with grotesque grins stretching across their near toothless mouths. At last some excitement. Foster 236 would make quick work of this newcomer. They felt not a trace of pity for the man even though they knew he had not done anything wrong—except to fall on the ruler of their wretched little world.

"Look pal," Rockson said, holding up both hands in a conciliatory gesture. "I don't want to take over your operation here or anything. Just let me find a nice little corner, nothing too big or fancy—and I'll just curl up there and you won't hear a peep out of me."

"You make jokes," Foster 236 said without a trace of a smile. "This not a funny place." He came slowly forward, all 359 pounds of him, on a 6' 7" frame so that he looked more like a walking table than a man. In his right hand he held the long blade, a stolen kitchen knife, which had already come within inches of Rockson's jugular. The flickering flame cast a sudden wave of light over the man's face and Rockson shuddered. The face was just a mass of scars. Whatever human features had once been there had long ago been swallowed up in cuts, slashes, punctures and burns. The man had obviously been through countless battles—and won.

"I am king here—me—" Foster 236 roared out in a blind fury. "No one touch me, no one." He came toward Rockson slicing the nearly 12-inch blade at the air, making little circles.

"Look fellow," Rock said, backing away, moving

instinctively into the quick deflect and counter-strike position he had developed over the years. "I really, really don't want to get into a fight. Because if we do, one of us will have to kill the other. Now, I don't have any particular reason to want to kill you. You seem like a nice enough fellow, and I'm positive that I don't feel like dying myself tonight as I'm too tired and too hungry to go into the next world. So how about we just relax." Rock held his hand out with as friendly an expression as he could muster.

Foster 236 lunged forward, the knife blade searching for Rockson's chest. But the Doomsday Warrior's fighting instincts had been honed to the sheer edge of perfection. His body turned in a split second as the steel came toward him. The huge body came forward as Rock stepped past the attacker and then swung his leg around catching the man's ankle. At the same moment he slammed down hard on the Slave King's shoulder. Foster 236 shot forward and down onto the concrete floor without even a second to stop himself. The entire momentum of his body had been directed by Rockson with the hand push/leg kick maneuver.

The huge body pulled itself up from the floor in a daze, the Slave King shaking his head trying to clear it. He stood up wobbling and the entire assemblage could see by the candlelight that his face was just a mass of blood. If there was room for any more wounds on that testament to slaughter called a face, another twenty or thirty gashes were added to the total and two more missing teeth. The nose had been broken so many times already that it was just a large lump of pliable cartilage. This particular fall had smashed it flat as a pancake, a pancake from which a syrup of blood poured to the floor. Foster 236 rose to his full height and once again hefted the blade, moving toward Rockson.

"Oh come on pal, do we have to go through more of this? *You're* the one getting roughed up—in case you hadn't noticed."

"I slipped scum—now you die!" He laughed a guttural snarl of contempt, half for Rockson and half for himself. Not one of the slaves had ever been able to challenge him. A few had tried but he had disposed of them within seconds. This one was different. But more than just a fight was at stake. With all the other slaves looking on, his power among them, all his "special" privileges—which consisted primarily of taking things whenever he felt so inclined—all were in jeopardy. And without that there was nothing.

Rockson sensed all this and again tried to give him a way out. "Look, let's just *say* you won—okay? All I want is to sleep."

"You will sleep," Foster smirked. He jumped forward with all of his immense weight with amazing speed for such a huge man. Rockson was caught slightly off guard. He managed to avoid the knife blade but Foster's full body weight caught him on the shoulder and the two men rolled over onto the floor with a resounding thud of over a quarter ton of combined flesh and muscle. Rock felt the tremendous bulk of his attacker slam onto his chest as his head whipped back against the concrete floor. He felt himself slipping under, into unconsciousness, yet just at the very moment that the darkness seemed about to fall, a light awakened his sense as some inner voice told him to come to—to move or he was dead.

It seemed like he had been out for minutes, in fact it was less than a second. Rockson opened his eyes to see the bulging eyes of Foster 236, and the knife hand high in the air about to begin its descent into his throat. The Doomsday Warrior pulled his head to the side as the blade fell like a guillotine and ricocheted off the hard floor. Rockson slammed up with his elbow directly beneath Foster's chin. The attacker flew up from the floor, nearly a yard into the air and then fell, landing on his knees. Rock rose in a flash and rushed over knowing this entire episode was not going to end in talk. As Foster rose to a standing position Rockson swung his right fist around in a roundhouse punch, from the Tam-tui system, letting it arc all the way around in a hidden orbit with his full body weight behind it. His steel-hard fist slammed into the side of Foster 236's head like a piston. The bleeding skull slammed back and forth on the bulldog neck like a vibrating gong and the narrow eyes closed as he sank slowly toward the floor. Rock let him have another one of the rocket-like punches from the other side as the unconscious body flew by. He didn't feel like having his newfound friend come and get him in the middle of the night. This would keep the fool out until morning. Foster's body hit the concrete like a toppling oak tree landing atop two bedraggled slaves who had been watching it all with great interest. The two squirmed out from under the elephantine weight and snatched their own little cardboard mattresses out of the way. It was clear that no one was going to elevate this whale of a man.

There was utter silence for a few seconds as every eye in the room zeroed in on Rockson who stood breathing hard, a huge bump welling up on the back of his lower skull where he had been struck.

"You are new bossman," one of the pitiful slave creatures, a man with no hair at all, even eyelashes, said. The others joined in a chorus of assent. Someone had to keep order, even if cruelly—otherwise they would all go at one another like wild beasts. The new fighter—he would be the leader. Perhaps he would be kinder than Foster 236.

"You leader," a wild-eyed man screamed.

"You new king," another said between drooling lips.

"King, king," they chanted, rising up from their filth-encrusted beds.

"No, no," Rock said, waving his hands with a bemused expression. First they tried to kill him—now they wanted him to rule them—all in the space of about two minutes. He saw a small empty spot by one of the window openings at the back end of the cement hut and walked over to it, rubbing his neck. The others followed behind, scampering around him, making animal grunts of excitement. Rock lowered himself down onto the 2×5 foot space, on each side of which grungy specimens were lying, their unwashed bodies sending out a somewhat pungent smell. But it would have to do. Rockson felt bone weary. He took off the field jacket he was wearing and made a pillow against the cracking wall. Then he lay back, settling into as comfortable a position as a human body could find, resting on two pieces of rough concrete. He put his hands behind his head and breathed out a deep sigh. It felt good just to not move after the marching of the last few days.

He heard sounds all around him and opened his eyes again in a flash, rising up ready to meet attack. But it was just the slaves, all 157 of them, surrounding him, their eyes trying to fathom this strange newcomer. He felt like he was in a goddamned zoo.

"Fuck off," he yelled, waving his arm. He made a fist and slammed it sideways against the wall which gave off a loud thud that echoed through the barracks. The slaves winced with fear and drew back, slowly settling into their own little sleeping squares. Within minutes all were asleep again in their own private hells.

Chapter Five

The Free Market, as it was called was a sprawling bazaar of large colorful tents a mile outside of Goerringrad. Those slaves not directly consigned to the labor crews were brought here to be sold to the highest bidder. Rona stared glumly down at her outfit as the flatbed truck tore down the last hill to the marketplace. Her hands were handcuffed behind her back and they had clothed her in a ridiculous pink semi-transparent harem skirt and a scanty bra that pushed her ample chest up and out. But it wasn't even her own situation that bothered her—it was Rock. Not knowing if he was alive or dead—if he was being eaten by the wild dog packs out there, all alone—it tore her apart. And there wasn't a goddamned thing she could do.

The wheezing truck came shooting down a winding lane, the driver blowing the horn to shoo dogs and children out of the way. As they came into the outer perimeter of the Bazaar, Rona looked around fascinated. Stalls selling every product imaginable were hawking their products—magic potions, candied lizards and snakes, furs, jewels, weapons, screaming out to all who passed by that "theirs" was the only place to shop. And between the stalls, magicians, dancers, snake charmers, men lying on beds of nails, or breathing fire. In spite of her captivity Rona watched in utter fascination. She had never seen anything quite like it.

They entered a main square where other slavers' trucks were parked and she was hustled off with other women prisoners and put into a waiting pen next to a raised platform which was to be the auction block. Outside, a loud gong rang and within minutes a crowd had gathered to start the bidding. She heard the auctioneer calling out in a singsong drivel of prices and bids. On top of the circular platform which was being slowly pulled around by three men below with ropes, was a young angelic-looking blond haired boy. A group of men in one section were eyeing the sullen youth with great interest. The auctioneer opened the boy's mouth and showed his teeth to the audience.

"See—good, strong. No disease." A grotesquely fat man in the audience, wearing tight pink body armor bid a hundred rubles. No one else raised and the fat man smiled lewdly, quickly took the lad into a waiting Sandrover and drove off.

"Next," yelled the bald headed, mustached auctioneer who seemed to speak 20 different languages at once as he engaged in super high-speed banter with the growing crowd of the rich, the powerful and the perverted. He pulled out three captured mountain women, strong featured, big-boned and muscled from their heavy work.

"Not the most beautiful slaves in the world, but good breeding stock. Very strong, work like ox." The bidding began at 50 rubles and worked its way up to 75. Finally they were sold to a stern-eyed farmer who looked as if he just might be thinking of using them as oxen.

"And now the *'piéce-de-résistance,'* " the auctioneer smiled down at the crowd, rubbing his hands together. "A prime fillet of womanhood—a mutant beauty. Once a princess in a strange land to the West, once in the harem of Ben-ali-Schwartz, but untouched. A virgin—"

Rona was pushed up the stairs by one of the market guards. Virgin, my ass, she half-snickered to herself. Rock would have something to say about that. The harem shoes were hard to walk in with their huge high heels.

There was a rumble of excitement in the crowd which had now swelled to several hundred. She stared down at them with a flashing anger. Slaves—slaves in the twenty-first century. Thus had the Communist "liberation" freed America.

"Here she is gentlemen—and not-so-gentlemen," the auctioneer snickered. Several Nazi officers and a KGB black-uniformed soldier nudged forward in the crowd. "Smile for our guests," the auction man said, giving her a sharp glance. Rona spit right in his face.

"Ah," he exclaimed wiping a dirty sleeve down his cheek, "a real tiger. Fit to be tamed by the most interesting methods. Do I hear the first bid? Let us start at 1,000 rubles." There were gasps from the audience. Many of the less well-dressed men were looking disconsolate. Others rifled through their wallets, sorry now that they had bought lesser quality merchandise already.

From a large sedan chair, a long thin hand with painted purple nails moved aside the silk curtain to let a single green eye peer out.

"I bid 2,000 rubles," a shrill voice croaked out.

"I hear 2,000–2,000–any better offers? Come now gentlemen–and ladies," he added, addressing the sedan chair's occupant. "This is as good as they get. This is–beauty." A Nazi in high black boots stepped forward.

"Might I touch?" he asked.

"Be my guest," the auctioneer replied, beaming. The Nazi walked up the stairs and opened Rona's mouth. She was still a little dazed from her drugging, but tried to bite, and missed. There was laughter from below as the chastened Nazi stepped back.

"I do not like being made ridiculous," he said coldly. "I will top that bid, and show this female what a man can do with a woman who defies him. Three thousand." It's going from bad to worse, Rona thought to herself. A fat man covered with golden necklaces and ruby bracelets pushed himself forward through the crowd. A jewel-encrusted dagger was stuck carelessly in the cumberbund of red silk.

"Please remove her bra," the jewel-bedecked man requested. The auctioneer yanked it down before Rona could twist away. If only she had her hands free. There were gasps from some of the audience.

"She has the white nipples."

"Bad luck," a man shouted at the back of the crowd and ran off, not looking back. Others withdrew their bids.

"Does the lady in the sedan chair top my bid?" the Nazi smiled. The chair was lifted by two black servants and carried quickly away. The auctioneer turned and angrily whispered to his assistant, "You fool! I told you to have her nipples rouged. In these parts white nipples are a hex sign. Sign of the witch! Someone with ESP who can make mincemeat of a man's will, of his sexual potency—" He turned back.

He turned back to the Nazi officer, instantly smiling fully again. "She is yours, for the bid you made."

"I am not superstitious," the German said. "I would like to add this woman to my rather odd collection. When she dies we can put her in the formaldehyde display tanks in my museum—with the others who defied me." Rona shuddered. A red stamp marked SOLD was inked on her forehead and the Nazi handed over his signature brand to the auctioneer who dipped it in acid and then pressed it against Rona's left forearm. It didn't hurt for a moment—and then the acid burned down below the epidermis. She screamed out in pain. When she could bear it, she looked down and read, "Property of Von Frueller," with a small Nazi swastika below it.

"Take her," the German said to two soldiers who accompanied him. They took Rona by her manacled arms and hustled her into a black Ziv limousine idling across the open center of the bazaar. They put a hood over her head. One way or another she seemed to be getting in the habit of falling into darkness.

Chapter Six

The after-effects of the Battle of Forrester Valley were being felt not just by Rona and Rockson and all the other captured Freefighters, but in Moscow as well. The full impact of the eradication of nearly two-thirds of the Nazi force he had sent over to destroy Century City and Ted Rockson, did not hit Premier Vassily, Ruler of All The World, until nearly three days later. Right in the middle of a reading by Rahallah, his irreplaceable servant and advisor, of Orwell's *1984*, the premier suddenly gagged and reached for his heart, unable to breathe and with a sharp pain ripping through his side.

Rahallah had expected it—a heart attack. The pills couldn't control his high blood pressure after the terrible defeat. The premier hadn't slept all night, despite massive use of sleeping pills. He hadn't even drunk his brandy that morning. The black African servant rose suddenly from his seat by the window as Vassily spasmed in his wheelchair, letting his heavy wool blanket spill onto the floor. His body arched up and he fell out toward the floor just as Rahallah got to him, catching the frail old body.

Rahallah pressed the intercom on the premier's desk, shouting for his doctors to come, and a stretcher. Within two minutes the premier of the Soviet Empire was on a rolling stainless steel table, being pushed toward the emergency operating room in the basement of his Kremlin home. An IV unit was stuck in his withered arm, dripping life-giving fluids into his bloodstream. The doctors tried everything, but to no avail. He seemed just too far gone this time. They left the O.R. and nodded "no" to Rahallah who waited anxiously outside.

"Is he still alive?" the tall, ebony faced servant, descended from African princes, asked.

"Yes, but barely," head surgeon, Mastrovich answered.

"Then I want all personnel to leave the operating room," Rahallah demanded. "I wish to be alone with the premier." The surgeon hesitated, but knew that as long as Vassily even clung to life, Rahallah's power as his right-hand was unquestionable.

"Yes sir," Mastrovich replied, feeling his lips almost tremble as he had to say it to a "nigger." But such were the rules of power.

While the doctors and the palace guards in their medal-festooned uniforms milled about in the corridor outside, Ruanda Rahallah, Son-of-the-Plains-Lion, master of the magic of his tribe, moved the rolling operating table toward the window of the O.R. where he pulled the thick drapes open so that daylight came streaming through. He opened the burlap bag he had brought with him from his quarters and took out its contents—robes, feathered hats, body paints, potions . . . Within minutes he was dressed in full tribal regalia, bright red paint on his face, white zebra stripes running down his arms and legs. He walked to the window, looked up at the brilliant blue skies and called on the Gods of the Lion to help him—to hear his words. He rattled a snakeskin-covered gourd filled with lion's teeth and chanted the incantations to Rukwanda, the Lion God of All Life.

"Oh Great Rukwanda, who roams the earth searching for souls to devour, hear my words. I, Son-of-the-Plains Lion, rightful heir to the throne of my tribe, son of your strength and courage. Oh hear me, devouring master . . ."

He dropped a handful of dried snake flesh into a large brass bowl he had set next to the motionless, pale body of Vassily, lying naked on the table and lit it. A pungent, acrid smoke rose up, covering the premier's face and chest. He walked around the dying man he had come to love and serve as his master and continued his chanting, shaking the gourd over Vassily, begging the Lion God to eat the evil spirits that had inhabited the premier.

The stainless steel door to the O.R. was open a crack, and from the spot that Czarina Alexandra had once stood, observing her husband's infidelities, the officers of the Elite Imperial Guard stood, their jaws dropped, listening to and watching the incredible sight. The premier, a sickly man who had suffered a stroke and was not expected to live an hour's time—and the African was doing *this*!

All the Kremlin was in chaos, as the black Rahallah continued to mumble chants and light bowls of powder around the failing body—in the very capital of the world—right in the Kremlin. Yet who dared challenge him? As long as the premier survived the black must be left alone. For Rahallah was greatly feared due to his influence over Vassily—and his black magic that had saved the premier once before, during "The Doctor's Plot." (*See Book #2*). Was the blackie a sorcerer? Could there be some ancient pagan power that this fearsome tall black man with his cool civilized demeanor had? Could the blackie himself be one of those demons which couldn't be killed?

The guards, and those jockeying for power in the event of the premier's death, watched as the primitive ritual continued. The premier should die. And when he did, this throwback, this black savage who dared flaunt his power in the very heart of the Russian empire, would die too, his head on a pole in front of the Supreme Soviet. Then the Politboro would doubtless be called into emergency session and unanimously elect Col. Killov, head of KGB in the USSA as the new premier. Killov-the-Strong, Killov-the-Feared. Killov, the human skeleton with the power and the cruelty to rule the world.

Rahallah jabbed his forearm repeatedly with the spike-sharp lion's tooth in his hand and let the wound drip down onto Vassily's chest. "This man must not die, Oh Great Lion God," he chanted in Swahili. "You must make him live, or my awful dream of evil will come true. The force of death—Col. Killov—will assume world power. And he will destroy the earth and all who inhabit it." For Rahallah knew that that was Killov's mission on earth—to end it all—to destroy the entire planet. Only then could his savage sexual lust for total power be satisfied. "O Lion hear me, grant my master's life to him for even one more year."

The next day, in the Kremlin building known as the Presidium, Vassily sat in his office, trembling—half drooling—in his wheelchair. Rahallah's treatment had worked—but only partially. He sat shaking, every nerve in his body vibrating wildly—but he was alive. Only the next few days would tell his fate. The premier listened to Rahallah read, for he liked to hear the articulate soft voice of the ebony man—it soothed him. His servant could tell that the premier was responding by an occasional nod of his head, and the thinnest of trembling smiles. Rahallah read from Robert Burns poems of love and peace. And peace though it seemed further away than ever was all that he prayed for.

There was one difference in the usual scene of the room-of-power. Vassily's wheelchair was not *behind* the marble-topped premier's desk—it was *alongside* the desk. And behind it sat Ruwanda Rahallah, who had been declared deputy premier, with all the powers of the office for the period that Vassily would be indisposed. Days before, when the premier had sensed that darkness was near, he had signed an Imperial Order, "I am hereby appointing Rahallah as deputy premier with all my powers—as long as I'm indisposed." Rahallah had objected but the premier had said, "They do not like you, but they fear me and they know you speak with the authority of my voice.

They will obey you—or they will fear for their own hides." Then he had added cryptically, "Trust no one."

Now, the premier was little more than a vegetable, and a black man in a white tuxedo sat behind the same desk that Peter the Great had given orders from. The generals, Politboro members, the petitioners from the many Soviet provinces who came to see Vassily were amazed—horrified—to see the black man sitting there, giving orders. But not a soul dared question him—not as long as Vassily survived.

Rahallah signed paper after paper, forging the premier's signature, which he had done many times in the past when Vassily's hands had been so wracked by arthritic pain that he couldn't move a finger. The next group in to see the premier was a contingent of military officials—from all the branches—whom Rahallah had ordered to join him in the premier's office. But Rahallah knew that the brass would not listen to him alone, so he rigged a small electric stimulator into Vassily's wheelchair. When he pressed a button hidden beneath the desk, the barely functioning premier would open his eyes, smile and nod yes. And Rahallah would need those signs of assent, for he was about to order a strike against KGB headquarters in his native country of Kenya. An all-out attack to wrest the province from the cruel rule of the KGB which had staked the country, and that of much of East Africa, for its own within years of the nuclear war a century earlier. Rahallah had tried for years to get the premier to agree to such a move. But the Grandfather would only tell him "someday Rahallah, someday—when our power is totally consolidated." But Rahallah could wait no longer for such a promised day. The premier might never recover, and Rahallah knew that when he went, so would he himself be burned in the funeral pyre. It could mean his life—but he would gladly give it if it meant freeing his homeland from the tyranny of a century.

But when the knock came at the door and one of the palace guard opened it, instead of generals and admirals, it was secret police chief Bukunin and six armed plain clothes men.

"What is the meaning of this?" Rahallah shouted, standing up to his full 6' 6" height.

"Orders of the New Committee for Proper Succession," Bikunin said smiling grimly. "You are removed from office on specific charges of—"

"Charges? What charges?" Rahallah asked, staring back at the usurper with cold dark eyes. "I occupy this office by virtue of the premier's proclamation."

"Ah yes, the proclamation, blackie. A proclamation acquired by the illegal use of sorcery! Sorcery is a crime against the state—it cannot exist under atheistic communism." He turned to his men, their cut-off subs hidden just beneath their large dark trenchcoats. "Remove this man to section B a Lubykana Prison." If Rahallah could pale he would have. Lubykana was nothing but an execution chamber—he would never return.

"Premier Vassily disapproves of this illegal interference of my carrying out his specific orders. Don't you Grandfather?" the black servant asked. He pressed the button beneath the desk. The premier appeared to wake up, as the slight electric charge surged through his central nervous system. His mouth grimaced open in what appeared to be a smile and then his head bobbed up and down several times as the neck muscles were stimulated. Rahallah released the button and the premier appeared to slowly close his eyes and sink back into sleep.

"See," Rahallah said imperiously, as a bead of sweat trickled down his forehead. "The premier orders you six men to arrest Comrade Bikunin—and all the conspirators involved in this New Committee—whatever that is. Immediately. Don't you Premier Vassily?" He pressed the button again—Vassily awoke and nodded, looking amazingly awake considering his true virtually unconscious state.

The guards looked at each other, frightened and confused.

"Do it!" Rahallah screamed out in the most threatening tones. The guards slowly turned their weapons toward their commander and took his weapon. Their fear of the power of the premier was greater than their fear of Bikunin. They would obey the Grandfather and Mother Russia.

"You," Rahallah said, pointing at the most intelligent looking of the secret police squad. "You are the new commander of the S.P. Premier Vassily will want a complete report on your rounding up of the conspirators by tonight. Put Bikunin in—Lubykana Prison." The African let a slight smile twitch across his face, as Bikunin went white as a sheet, his lips unable to even talk. The guards took him at gunpoint from the room.

Rahallah collapsed back into the chair. This couldn't go on for long like this. Hours—days. The entire Russian command was doubtless, plotting how to get rid of Rahallah—and kill the badly weakened premier. Somehow Rahallah had to buy time, for himself and the premier. They'd have to get out of the country until he regained—if ever—his powers. But how? How could he assert his power, consolidate his position and make it appear that the premier was still in power, yet be safe? The answer came to him in a flash. He would go the USSA—a fact finding mission with the premier. He would call a summit, with Col. Killov and President Zhabnov. He would tell them it was to bury the hatchet between the Red Army and KGB forces—to get their real enemy—Ted Rockson, the Doomsday Warrior. He was the one man that could bring them all together. Rockson was the key. Rockson—who had blown up the ICBM Missile Control base in Moscow; Rockson who had destroyed their invading Nazi army in the Rocky Mountains; Rockson who had scarred the pale face of the mad Killov just months before; Rockson who had humiliated President Zhabnov right in the Oval Office of the White House. That would be the summit's reason. And at the same time, it would get Rahallah and the premier away from all these plotters. Away from the New Committee.

Chapter Seven

He was dreaming—strange, twisted thoughts weaving in and out of his mind like a crazy quilt pattern of half-forgotten images, faces, battles. He saw a city, an incredible city beneath the ground filled with futuristic architecture, lighting, computerized machinery. But just for fleeting seconds, as the images were whizzed across his mind like a swarm of burning meteors, visible for a moment and then vanished into the very air.

He saw faces—a woman with long flowing red hair, and another woman, blonde, with blue eyes as clear as a still pond on midsummer's day. His heart filled with aching for both of them—yet who were they, their names, their places in his life—he knew nothing. The dreams lasted through the night, torturing him as the part of his unconscious that knew the past tried desperately to get through to him.

He was dreaming of a man, a Chinese man, who fought with him. But they were not trying to harm one another, just learn from their contests. The man was his friend. Rockson again felt a surge of love and then terror as he had no idea who the man was or if he really had ever met him. They were sparring, the man's hands whirling like a windmill in front of his eyes. Rockson felt something hit his shoulder and he parried.

Suddenly voices were rising around him. The Doomsday Warrior opened his eyes to see three Nazi guards, their rifles aimed at his chest. A fourth guard lay on the floor wiping a trickle of blood from his lip.

"You fool," the man said, rising, "what do you mean striking me? I could have you shot this very second."

"I apologize," Rockson said as he rose slowly to a standing position not wanting to meet his fate, as if he was about to, lying down on his back. "I was dreaming—and had a nightmare and I thought you—" The German officer lashed out with a swagger stick he held in his right hand, slamming Rockson across the face, so that a two-inch gash appeared in the Doomsday Warrior's thick mutant skin and a line of red ran down his cheek. The officer seemed satisfied with that, and told his men to uncock their weapons.

"He will not repeat such an error again, I assure you of that," the officer said, addressing the slaves in the room. "Nor any of you, I dare say. Now go. You men, go to your morning departure station—the new ones who came in last night come with me." The S.S. officer led Rockson and four of the other captured Freefighters, their chains still around their ankles, down the main road to the central square of the fortress, where nearly three hundred other recently arrived slaves were lined up having their chains removed and being branded with name and number. As they approached Rockson heard a spine-tingling high-pitched wavering sound, blasting out from speakers mounted around the square. With a start he realized it was someone screaming—a human being screaming for his very life. The voice rose and fell, occasionally begging for mercy before it resumed the terrifying animal shrieks of ultimate pain.

"What are those?" Rock asked the guard, who turned to him with an angry expression as if affronted that a slave had dared to ask him a question.

"That is the Screamer, scum. Each day, one of the slaves who has caused trouble is taken to the House of Pain and tortured. Tortured most horribly. Those are his screams. You will hear them a lot, scum. They will remind you of what happens to those who go against the rules and order of the Fourth Reich." The guard paused. "And scum, do not dare to ask me or any other German officer a question again. It will be your last."

Nearly a hundred S.S. guards surrounded the prisoners with their Kalashnikovs at the ready. The machine gun posts mounted on towers throughout the fortress city were trained on them from six different towers that ringed the square. Rockson's leg chains were at last unlocked and he was led to the next line where two fat S.S. slugs sat in chairs, electric branding irons in their hands. As each man passed, he was given his new name, which was simultaneously burned into his flesh forever.

"Smith 27," sizzle.

"John 52," sizzle.

"Herbert 75," sizzle. The scent of smoking flesh filled the air, giving off a sweet smell almost of pork. At last it was Rockson's turn and he looked down, not even averting his head as the portly brander yelled out, "Joe 113," and slammed the white hot tab of electric fire with the words "Joe 113" onto Rockson's forearm. The Doomsday Warrior didn't flinch from the pain but let it enter his body as a source of pure energy. He would use the pain, the anger from it to fuel him. He wanted to remember it so that perhaps some day he could return the favor.

When the unlocking and branding procedures had been completed, the new slaves were lined up in rows at one side of the square. A tall platinum blond man came swiftly down a row of stairs from the largest building in the fortress city—the S.S. Headquarters. He wore his full dress uniform, black, creased in razor-sharp lines, black boots kneehigh, and the dark general's cap with its single lightning bolt with "S.S." on each side.

"I am General Kohl of the S.S. This is the only time you will ever see me. If I should see you again it will be only to look down on your dead face. You are slaves of the glorious Soviet/Nazi forces. Your lives are now devoted to the construction of this city. You may die now if you wish—just step forward and my men will be glad to send you on your way. If you wish to live, work. Work harder than you've ever worked in your life. I do not promise you a long life, but I do promise you death if you do not keep working. It is simple. If you entertain any absurd thoughts of escaping, let me inform you that there are nearly one hundred machine gun towers around this fortress, sheets of barbed wire, and beyond, mine fields. No one has escaped from here alive. Many have tried. Their rotting remains are in the swamps."

He looked them over, trying to instill the fear of his very soul into every one of them. Fear was what drove these slaves, drove them like workhorses, like lifeless machines—the fear of guaranteed death should they not be able to work their quotas. It seemed to work very well as motivation, very well indeed.

"Goodbye then," the general said, pursing his

shrunken, almost white lips together. "And remember—you are contributing to a great cause, are being given the opportunity to do something worthwhile with your wretched lives." He saluted the guards and turned, heading quickly back up into the S.S. building, with two truck-sized flags hanging limply outside, immense swastikas emblazoned in black on their blood-red fabric.

"Move on," the guards said, breaking the men down into the units they would be working in. Rockson and the twenty men around him were shuffled off to Work Group G, which lined up at one side of the square. Trucks poured out of nowhere and down onto the main avenue and the slave laborers were loaded into the big dark green transport vehicles.

They drove down the main road and toward the back of the fort, passing row after row of storage buildings, then Nazi troop barracks and at last their own slave quarters on the outer edges. Rockson looked down at the blackened burning skin on his forearm and the words JOE 113. It was as good a name as any, he thought ironically. It would do for now. The truck suddenly lurched to a stop and the men were ordered out by the guards at the back.

"This is a garbage detail," a young pimply-faced German lieutenant said to them in as officious and condescending a tone as he could muster, though his voice cracked every once in a while. "You are the waste of the waste, the scum of the scum," the lieutenant addressed them, his red pimples covering his face like little volcanos about to erupt against the chalky whiteness of his skin.

"You are here to carry the waste products out of this

fortress," the lieutenant continued, walking back and forth in front of them. Off to his side stood another fifty or so men, those who already worked on the G-squad. "Some men considered it quite fortunate to end up here. When they move the refuse, the food, the bodies, the excrement, to the swamps to the west of the Fortress, they can eat what they can find. The men of the garage squad are the fattest men of all the slaves. So you see perhaps you are quite fortunate to be the scum of the scum." He stood up to as imperious a height as he could at 5' 2" tall, wet his lips with a narrow tongue, and continued. "It is of no concern to me what you savages eat. All I demand of you is that the work get done. That each night whatever is here in this disposal sector is empty by nightfall. Then you and I will get along just fine and you can, as they say, have your cake and eat it too.

"My final words—you are the only slaves of the city who go outside the walls. Thus you will think no doubt of escape. Don't. There are nearly twenty guards who will always be with you. They will kill you on the spot, without hesitation for the slightest infraction. Believe me. If you should somehow get away you would find, I'm afraid, nothing but radioactive swampland stretching for nearly fifty miles. Impenetrable. No man who has disappeared into its innards has ever returned." The lieutenant looked around, decided he had said enough and turned on his heels back to his staff car, driving quickly off from the wretched smell that the piles of waste and bodies gave off as they festered in the slowly rising sun.

"You," one of the guards said, pointing to Rockson and the ten men around him, "over there to the B-squad." The Doomsday Warrior's stomach almost turned when he looked inside a long steel dumpster and saw its load. Dead slaves from the past two days, taken from where they had fallen and just deposited here. The fortress, with somewhere between 5,000 and 6,000 slaves—they had lost count—lost nearly 200 of them a day, so rigorous was the work load they carried, so little the allowance for rest. The corpses were piled one atop another inside the rectangular garbage disposal like bloody dolls. Their faces and pale white bodies were already ballooning up, bloating from their own rotting flesh and the gases they produced. The bodies were all naked—the clothes were recycled—not the humans. And Rockson could see as he looked closer that the flesh was crawling with insects, ants, roaches, centipedes, small yellow and pink worms—all taking their fill.

"Here," a voice said brusquely. Rockson turned; one of the slaves, a large man nearly his own size, was handing him a rusted and slightly bent pitchfork.

"What the hell is this for?" Rockson asked, not too pleased with the budding thought of what in fact they were to be used for.

"For loading, what the hell do you think, scum," the man snarled back. "Listen, I heard about you already. You're the troublemaker who fought with Foster 236 over in block R17. I don't care about that, but just don't cause no trouble here, okay? I'm Smith 679. I'm the work boss of this gang. The Nazis hold *me* responsible for whatever goes down. Now I don't give a shit about anyone but myself. You understand. I'm out for me—for every scrap of food, every bit of favor I can get from the Nazi pigs. Anything—any man, gets in my way, threatens my power—he's dead. All I got to do is tell our friends over there that you're causing problems and they'll shoot you on the spot." He looked Rockson up and down, a little surprised by the calm motionless way that Joe 113 listened to the words without betraying the slightest emotion.

"Understand?" Smith 679 asked, not quite able to bring himself to look right into those throbbing eyes, but focusing on his forehead instead.

"Sure," Rockson spat out, becoming more disgusted by the minute by everyone in this damned hellhole. God, what his fellow Americans had sunk to, he thought. The way these slaves dressed, letting their clothing just disintegrate around them. They let themselves *be* slaves—helped the Reds and the Nazis carry out their plans of subjugation, humiliation and death. It was as if they had all just given up from the start—said here we are, signed, sealed and delivered, do what you want with us. Why, if every slave in the complex suddenly fought back, they could probably defeat the Germans or at least destroy the fortress. He felt a stirring in his breast to make them understand, to change the way they acted and thought. To change them from slaves into men. But how in hell he would ever do that he hadn't the slightest idea.

"All right, let's get this show on the road," Smith 679 roared out to the other corpse disposers, who stood around listlessly, their gray and brown rags hanging to the ground like the fallen branches of a dead tree. The head of the corpsemen walked to the back of the dumpster and unhitched a large clasp, swinging the ten-foot square steel door open with a resounding clank as it hit the outer side.

"Bring the train," Smith 679 ordered. From around the side of a large flat square concrete structure men came pushing a flatbed railroad car, stripped of everything except its wheels and wooden top. Rockson looked around and suddenly noticed that there were two sets of railroad tracks that ran through the garbage sector and off toward the west.

"Load 'em up," Smith 679 roared out as the flatbed came alongside the open end of the dumpster from which bodies were already sliding in bloody trails onto the ground.

Two slaves in front of Rockson leaned over and dug their pitchfork into two of the falling dead, spearing them in the chest or stomach. They pulled back as hard as they could and heaved the things up and onto the railroad car, where they landed with loud spattering sounds. Rockson took a deep breath and lanced one—a large-bellied fellow with folds of fat that had formed breasts on his chest, now half rotted away. With all his strength the Doomsday Warrior hefted the thing in a perfect arc up from the ground and over to the train, where it slammed down with a squishing thud.

The slaves forked their way through the smorgasboard of dead until the train was loaded—bodies, arms, white legs drained of their blood, dangling over the sides.

"Get behind it, all of you," Smith 679 ordered. His voice screamed, the veins in his throat popping out whenever he gave an order, as if he had to frighten his charges at every moment of contact with them. The twenty new men of the corpse squad lined up around the back and sides of the nearly 60-foot long flatbed, Rockson taking the middle back end.

"Heave, heave," Smith screamed out, standing alongside the death car, waving his arms up and down in an effort to make them put some strength into it. The hardest part was just getting the immense momentum of the thing going. It felt to the slaves as if they were pushing against a mountain. Not a budge, but as they heaved and grew beet-red with exertion, slowly, an inch at a time, the thing rolled achingly forward. First an inch each second, then a foot, until suddenly it was sliding forward as its great bulk took over. Now they just had to keep the energy going, running alongside it, pushing with outstretched arms. It was nearly a mile and a half to the outer edge of the swamp where the corpses were to be dumped. The land was flat and the car filled with newly dead raced along as if to an impotant meeting.

"Why the hell don't they use an engine?" Rockson asked the slave pushing next to him, a tough-looking fellow, but with a reasonably friendly face.

"Don't want to waste the fuel," the man spat, as he ran pushing from behind, bent over at an almost 50-degree angle. " 'Sides, it gives them something for us to do—and they don't have to get all involved in the stench and all."

"Thanks," Rock answered, grateful to even get a normal human response from one of these cold and hostile slave workers. Smith 679 and the guard team rode alongside in a small truck, also without sides, watching with bored expressions, their Kalashnikovs on their laps. They had seen the same sight for months and it no longer disgusted or even amused them. It was just work, until they could return to their air-conditioned barracks and eat and watch the films that the base provided. For there were elite troops, every one of them the proud flagbearers of the resurgent Nazi army—that at least in the back of the minds of all the Germans here in the USSA might one day once again become the supreme forces. But these were thoughts they never expressed to their Red commanders and suppliers. They were firmly under Premier Vassily's control. But someday, someday. . . .

"Slow down," Smith 679 screamed out through a small cardboard megaphone he always carried with him. He could see the foaming green and purple scummed swamp just a few hundred yards ahead. There was protective concrete stopgate about five feet from the edge but all he needed was for the fools to go too fast and slam right through. His private room, his real food—scraps from the officer's canteen—all would be gone. His life he cared little about, it was the privileges, the power over the others. *That* was his only purpose, his only reason for life.

The slaves stopped pushing and ran alongside the gradually slowing death car, reaching out with extended hands when it grew closer to the swamp and pulling back now, trying to stop the great load of carcasses. They eased the freight in so the car stopped just a foot from the concrete embankment.

"Excellent, excellent," Smith 679 said, jumping from the truck with as much of a smile as his greedy rodent-like face could exhibit. All his worries of losing his "wealth" vanished like clouds of a thunderstorm blown away—at least for today.

He walked over to the swamp and looked in. It seemed all right today. Sometimes it bubbled and seemed to almost writhe with releasing gasses and decomposing matter. Every bit of waste that the fort produced was dumped here—from the bodies to the rotting food of the officers to the excrement, used chemicals, and by-products of their science and production labs. It stretched on for miles, thick as pea soup but never smooth, always covered with a surface of thick, bubbling foam with the tops of things dumped in recently still poking through from place to place—the roof of a wrecked car, a leg . . . God knew how deep the thing was—but so far, at least, it seemed to be able to swallow everything they could give it. Only strange narrow black-barked trees with red leaves and purple vines running down their trunks seemed able to grow in the foulness. They stood every fifty, hundred feet or so in little groves of ten or twenty, rising right out from under the impenetrable green oily muck below them.

"Okay—dump 'em!" Smith 679 yelled out, walking the ten feet over to the railroad car. The men formed a line and walked down to the side of the car, each one in turn spearing the closest body on the flatbed on the tip of his long, curved pitchfork. Each man hoisted the thing with all his upper-body strength so that he was holding it almost upright some four or five feet straight over his head, and walked with lurching steps toward the edge of the swamp where he let the pitchfork fall forward so that the body splashed into the thick slime and disappeared instantly beneath the surface.

Rockson's fork tore into a frail-looking elderly man with a long silver beard. The man's naked body looked almost child-like without hair. He couldn't have lasted very long in a Nazi workgang, Rockson thought to himself as he lifted it overhead and walked over to the bank. He let the man fall down and watched with a tightening sensation in his stomach as the body, that rigor mortis piece of nothing that had once been a man with a real life, was disposed of like the most wretched piece of refuse. He vowed to wreak revenge for all the dead right then and there. Somehow, he, whoever the hell he was, would make the murderers pay—in blood. And he also knew, whoever he was, that he was the kind of man who would do what he vowed.

His next corpse must have been ten days old, as it seemed ready to come apart at the proverbial seams of the shoulder and thigh at any moment. Rockson hefted it carefully, but as he jerked it overhead one of the legs fell off and landed on his shoulder, flopping onto the ground with a slapping dead sound. Rock watched the limbless body plunge into the green swamp and then, with a look of infinite disgust, speared the chalk-white leg with dark green veins running along each side and hefted it over into the muck. It had just hit the foam and slid in, when Rock felt himself grow faint. Voices, images, crashing in his head. He couldn't understand them, but they hurt—burning like shrapnel ripping through his skull. He felt himself falling, falling, being pulled toward a cacophonous chorus of madness. Suddenly an arm was pulling him. Rock opened his eyes and looked up into the grimy face of the friendly slave he had talked to behind the railroad car.

"Mister you was almost just dead," the man said, pulling Rock back and letting him go, as he saw the man could stand on his own. "You was halfway down into that swamp," the slave continued with a half grin on his face, "eyes rolling up in your head and all. I just happened to be behind you and . . ."

"Thanks," Rock said, with a smile. He owed his life to

the man. "What's your name?"

"Tom 72," he said, then leaned forward, relaxing. "Real name's Calvin Windbinder."

"Pleased to meet you, Mr. Windbinder. I'm afraid I don't even know my real name, so for the moment just call me Joe 113."

"Well you watch out mister. Life ain't worth a lip of soggy spit around here. They'd just as soon watch you go in as not. Even the other slaves. Me—I guess I ain't given up on being a human being yet. No matter how bad things are." He turned and headed back to the line of body movers, carrying the long blood-spattered pitchfork loosely in one hand. Rock stepped back from the endless miles of green swamp and scanned it with his keen eyes. The voices—very dim and moving off. What the hell were they? Why could he hear them and no one else? Nothing made sense to him. He was a stranger even in his own flesh.

Chapter Eight

Rona had the hood removed from her eyes only after she was hustled into a car and taken to an immense building several miles away. The air conditioning inside hit her like a brick. It was hot and moist outside, but inside arcticly cool. Only high officers would have such costly temperature controls. She looked around. She was in a marble hall, the foyer to the cylindrical-shaped building above her. The walls were covered with swastikas and a huge banner with Hitler's face.

There were footsteps coming down a flight of stairs ahead—it was the man who had bought her, walking with another even higher-ranked German, an ugly scarred man with a black eyepatch over one eye, a strange covering that seemed to be made of multifaceted glass.

"Ah yes, I see," the eye-patched Nazi said to his second-in-command, "you have not lied, she is quite beautiful indeed." He put his hand on her chin and turned her face this way and that. "Such fine classical features—like an ancient Aryan goddess. Yes, yes, we must check her." He turned to the guard to his right. "Kurt, bring the templates up to my office." The man clicked his heels and rushed off. The guards hustled Rona along behind the Nazi high commander, over to the elevator and then up to a plush office suite on the 9th floor. "There," the eye-patched German told her to sit on a red velvet sofa. She glared at him, but was glad to rest and sat down.

He seemed to be nervous as he sat several feet away and kept staring at her with a peculiar expression on his hard face. She looked about the room to avoid his steel gaze. There was of course, the picture of Hitler lit with its own track lighting. The Fuhrer was dressed as a Teutonic knight in shiny armor, astride a strong Germanic-looking steed. Behind him cities burned and beneath the horse's front hooves, someone with a long nose and money falling from a purse—was being crushed—a Jew, no doubt. The usual Nazi bullshit, she thought as she scanned the rest of the room.

There were immense oil paintings depicting stars, galaxies, and a number of astrological symbols. Yes, she remembered that the Nazis were deeply into the movement of the stars, as Hitler had been. Deeply into the forces of destiny and the collective racial unconscious. Ideas like reincarnation, predestination, racial memory—all these were accepted by the Germans in some twisted sort of way. In the way that the Iron Cross was used by them—a symbol of Christ—but perverted, twisted. They knew nothing of real spirituality, the way of inwardness, the way of meditation. Instead they had chosen a pseudo-religious Nazi religion of purity that justified their genocide against the Jews, the gypsies, the Buddhists—anyone who didn't fit the Nazi mold.

She turned to the largest illuminated oil painting on the wall to her left and gasped. A tuxedoed Adolph was sitting in a Victorian chair, calm, in control, fatherly. And half-lying at his feet was Eva Braun. Not the mousey Eva Braun, Hitler's mistress, that Rona had seen old file photos of in Century City's archives, but a greatly idealized, perfect Eva Braun. She had reddish-blonde locks down to her bare very ample breasts—breasts with tiny pink nipples. Eva sat absolutely naked, long-leggedly stretched out looking up at her man, the Fuhrer. Rona realized that Eva's face reminded her not of the real Eva Braun but of someone else. Then she nearly gasped—it was her own face. And that full body, strong and big-boned, yet graceful, sexual like a cat—it was Rona's!

No wonder the Nazi officer was looking at her so strangely. He sat under the portrait every day, daydreaming, thinking of the glorious German past.

"Please be comfortable," the German suddenly spoke up. "What is your name?"

"My real name is for my friends only," the Freefighter replied coldly. A decanter was rolled over to her on a serving table by one of Von Reisling's underlings.

"Care for some sherry? Perhaps some schnapps?" he asked, trying to sound his most civilized.

"Nein," she snarled.

"German? Very good. How much do you speak, beautiful woman?" She let him have a string of insults. The German language hypnotapes, the Freefighters had listened to in Century City before the battle of Forrester Valley had been quite efficient. The eye-patched officer reddened noticably.

"So fluent . . . and so vile . . . but you interest me." Von Reisling stood up, admiring her figure, long and lean yet so full.

"Guard, have the skull templates arrived?"

"Jawohl, mein commandant," the soldier replied, handing over the device, designed by the Germans to measure racial characteristics. Von Reisling took them and then ordered the soldier out.

"Remove yourself, but first check her ankle and hand restraints. This woman appears to be problematic." The guard checked the cuffs and left, closing the door behind him.

"My name is Von Reisling. General Von Reisling. Perhaps you have heard of me?" the German officer asked.

"Why should I have?" Rona answered coldly.

"I am in charge of this area of the U.S.S.A. As a matter of fact, it has been ceded to me. This is to be the seat of the Fourth Reich—the new Germany." He opened his desk and took out a long sharp dagger and approached her. "Relax," hc said with a dark smile, "I only wish to remove your garments. These silly clothes will have to be cut off. A woman like you should be seen fully to be appreciated. I will arrange proper dress for you later." He began cutting off her sheer clothing and she couldn't do a thing to stop him. He took his time, pausing and half gasping as he sliced away the red halter top. The fullness of her white tipped breasts came free.

"Such a wonderful roundness," he said. "Like a German goddess." He reached out to touch her, squeezing the flesh fruits between his icy fingers. "Ah, let us see the rest," he said with a hoarse whisper, drawing back. He continued to cut away at her garments which fell to her feet, until the only thing she had on were the sparkling red high heel shoes. He stood up and admired her.

Then he walked over to the desk to the pile of labelled templates—cutout profiles of the "Ideal Aryan Woman." He picked up the first one, carefully placed it against her silhouette.

"Hmm, not quite—but that's type six, the lowest. Let's skip to number three." Still it didn't match. There was one last template left and he fitted it against her face—and gasped. "Eva Braun," he cried out. "You are the reincarnation of Eva Braun!" He stepped back from her, a mixture of seething desire and fear on his pale face.

Rona suddenly had a hunch. If she was a goddess, then he was a mere mortal. Perhaps she could use it to her advantage.

"Yes, I am Eva Braun, Hitler's wife whom he married just before shooting himself—and me—in the Berlin bunker in 1945. How dare you treat me like this!" she spat out. "I have put up with your stupid insults, your coarseness long enough." She glared at him, trying to work some of the ESP thought-influencing that Rock had shown her, trying to reach into the German's mind to make him fear her.

"Now, kneel before me, cur. Properly show your respect." Von Reisling grew white, his one good eye fixed like glue to her glaring green eyes that were so dominant, so . . . He fell to his high booted knees, and crawled the distance to her along the floor. It's working, Rona thought, though even she was amazed at how well.

"Now, show your respect," she commanded. The Nazi leader began licking the fronts of her high heels, then her ankles.

"Just the shoes, insolent one," she demanded in as haughty a tone as she could muster.

"Yes, my goddess, yes. Just to kiss your shoes. Yes, yes . . ." She let him grovel and slobber at her feet for a while while she tried to think of what to do next.

Within hours Rona was unbound, bathed in milk and dressed in a golden robe, classical Greek style as Eva Braun wore in many of the idealized paintings of her. She was given silk slippers and two handmaidens and taken to a vast, white-draped room on the top floor of the cylindrical building that was Von Resling's headquarters. From her barred window she surveyed the city of Goerringrad, only six months old but growing in leaps and bounds as money was poured in from Vassily in Moscow. Down and to her left she saw the slave market where she had been sold just hours before. Now she was here, in a palace, a living goddess, to be worshipped. Fate handed out strange surprises. If she could just somehow use her position to find Rockson, to kill these Nazi swine. But she felt suddenly achingly tired and lay her red tresses on the satin pillows of her bed. The two maids came and tucked her in, and then sat near her, watching as the goddess slept.

But the news the next morning was sobering. Yes, she was Eva Braun, reincarnated goddess. They wouldn't harm her. They would feed her, let her sleep, let her do anything, the gold-robed Nazi priest said, "anything accept leave." A living goddess was to be worshipped. She might spend the rest of her life comfortably, with perfumed servants, with ethereal gowns, untouched, a virgin. But she could never leave. Never.

All that day, high Nazi officers came to see her and fall at her feet. Von Reisling too, came twice, begging her to let him once again kiss her bare feet. She kicked him in the face when he tried. But her physical and verbal abuse of the Nazi ruler seemed to only increase his affections for her. For he had found—in his mind—the one, the perfect woman. And he wished to be punished by her.

The high priest came again that night, trying to get her to cooperate more with her new role as goddess incarnate, telling her what an honor it all was, and that she would come to realize how privileged she was, come to understand her obligations to the Reich. He gave her a picture of Hitler to sleep with—a three-dimensional picture of the short, mustached murderer with that constant stern look.

When the priest left, she spat on it and threw it into the corner where it split into pieces. Suddenly her new vocation as Nazi goddess didn't seem to hold too many possibilities—it was a prison. A prison from which she might never escape.

Chapter Nine

Colonel Killov smirked as the nervous butler delivered him his vegetable juice laced with megavitamins. This butler was new—the old one, Georgi, had dropped a saucer on Killov's lap the week before. Georgi did not survive the experimental intestinal transplant surgery performed on him that same night. This butler was truly Germanic looking. It would look good, when Von Reisling came, Killov thought, to show Aryan servants waiting upon me. To show the Nazi Commander that *all* men—even Nazi leaders—must bend to his will.

And why not, the KGB leader mused as he dismissed the pale faced butler with a wave of his heavily veined skeletal hand. I am a superman too. Perhaps I've lost some weight due to the obligations of my high office of late. He looked in the mirror and then quickly away as what he saw didn't quite fit his concept of an Aryan god. The many pills he took to keep himself going had escalated over the last year until he was an addict, using as many as 30 different pills a day—ups, downs, tranquilizers, euphorics—he had lost count. His body had shrunken down to just under 90 pounds and his face had grown gaunt as a skull, hence the name "The Skull" had been given to him, by those who served under him—never of course, spoken to his face.

But if Killov was not the prettiest of those vying for power in the world of 2089 A.D., he was the most ruthless and clever—a master of double-dealing strategy. He had managed to make contact with the Supreme Nazi commander in the United Socialist States of America, Von Reisling, and convince him that Premier Vassily had never meant for the Nazi invasion to succeed, but to be wiped out here in the radioactive mountains of Colorado. And once he had planted the seed of doubt, of betrayal, in the German's mind, he had been able to lure him over to his side—and along with him nearly 150,000 highly trained commandos. Just the kind of force that Killov could use to take on Premier Vassily, through his lackey, Zhabnov and the Red Army forces here in America. Von Reisling had hesitated for a time, but the stupid battle plans of Vassily had resulted in the destruction of nearly two-thirds of the proud German army and his panzer divisions. But once convinced, the eye-patched general was eager to have his remaining troops join Killov's KGB Death Squads. He would throw in his lot with "The Skull" rather than go back to Germany defeated, a coward.

Killov called his helipilot Sarmonsky and ordered him to ready a flight to Goerringrad. Within minutes he was flying off from his Denver monolith, the

KGB headquarters, and off to the newly built Nazi Fortress City of Goerringrad. He was impressed with the amount of construction they had been able to throw up in just months. If he could just tap that fanatic Nazi energy he could have the world.

The chopper landed in the center of a clearing with a swastika burned into the grass. Then the red carpet was literally rolled out for Killov, along with all the amenities of supreme command—twenty-one gun salute, goosestepping Nazi troops, the requisite reviewing of the honor guard. Von Reisling in sparkling patent leather riding boots came eagerly forward. He kissed Killov—with a hidden grimace—on both cheeks, so sunken and discolored. My God, Von Reisling thought to himself, the man was like a living skeleton, almost without real flesh at all.

"Thank you comrade, for coming here," the Nazi leader said, saluting stiffly. Were it not for the pressing affairs of the Fourth Reich I, of course, would have come to you. But for the moment, you are my honored guest." Killov mouthed a stiletto smile.

"Let's get down to business Von Reisling. You have, I assume three drafts of the agreement worked out between us by our staffs?"

"Yes," Von Reisling replied firmly. "Typed in triplicate for our final signatures. It's in my office." They went into the 10-story stainless steel tower that housed Von Reisling's staff.

"My men will bring them in to us," Von Reisling said. "But first, I insist that as my guest, you share in German hospitality. Here, this way." He took Killov gently by the arm, a gesture which the KGB commander, who hated to be touched, pulled slightly back from, but continued to let the Nazi guide him. Together, two of the most powerful and ruthless men in the world walked into Von Reisling's ornately decorated dining room. They seated themselves at the table, covered with embroidered white linen and a waiter poured them each a glass of sherry. A needless time waster, Killov thought, but it *was* protocol to drink before signing anything important.

"To the great American Reich that is now born. And to its visionary leader—Fuhrer Von Reisling," Killov said, clinking glasses with the eye-patched general.

"And to the new president of the U.S.S.A. and someday premier of all the world, Commander Killov," Von Reisling said returning the toast.

Killov merely skimmed the two-page treaty set before him by an underling. It hardly mattered what it said, since the KGB colonel had no intention of honoring it beyond what was needed to carry out his plans. Then he would destroy Von Reisling without hesitation. There were enough ambitious men already vying for the earth's rule—he didn't need another one. Especially not one with such a strong force as the German. He quickly penned in his signature as did Von Reisling. They smiled crocodile smiles at one another and then toasted again. At last Killov said he must be off and Von Reisling replied how sorry he was that they could not enjoy each other's company any longer.

The KGB commander walked back to his wasp-shaped black command chopper and ordered his pilot to take off at high velocity from the wretched city. Killov began shaking from the tension of the meeting and quickly took out two arthovalium pills to charge up his tired body. The pills gave him a certain sexual charge, hot sensations that streamed through his body, bringing a smile to the tight face. A sexual thrill he could not get from his missing testicles—the ones he had never been born with. He would use Von Reisling for a time, let the proud Nazi be his stooge, until it was time to topple him along with Vassily and Zhabnov. And that moment was drawing closer every day.

Closer even than he realized as he heard the news relayed to his chopper as it flew back to Denver. "The premier has had a stroke," his Intelligence chief back at the Monolith broadcast. "He is not expected to live beyond the next few hours."

Killov smiled so broadly that his thin dry lips cracked in the middle, emitting a trickle of brownish blood, half coagulated.

"Wonderful news," he muttered to the pilot. "Now we will see how long the fatman Zhabnov can avoid fulfilling my vow to roast him like a pig on the White House lawn. I will garnish the pig with his own precious rose petals from his garden, then feed his meat to the dogs—and those who supported him."

"Yes sir, yes sir," the pilot nodded vigorously to his supreme commander, terrified to even look him in the eyes. For Killov at that moment with his translucent skin, his eyes filled with murderous madness, his face as narrow as a skull, looked like nothing less than death itself—searching for souls to take back to hell.

Chapter Ten

The days dragged on like funeral dirges for Rockson and the other slaves. Each day they were awakened at six from their hovels and sent out to work—work for 10 hours, break for a quick meal of nearly rancid gruel, then work for another six hours before being sent back to their barracks, passing the nightfeeding station at the gate of the slave sector of the fortress, where they were given a bowl of potatoes and a slice of bread. It was not exactly a paradise on earth. And for Rockson and his work crew of the corpse squad, an endless procession of bodies. After a while they blurred together, just white bloody sacks of rotting flesh. All traces of their humanness, their personalities vanished beneath their cold flesh.

Whenever the Doomsday Warrior worked at the swamp he felt the strange sensations again. It was as if he were listening in on a conversation between dozens of creatures all screaming in some foreign language and broken with a fuzzy static. It made him dizzy, draining some part of his senses that he couldn't even locate. So he was extremely careful when unloading bodies into the swamp, making sure that he never was within calling distance of the mysterious voices. The swamp just kept taking all that they dished in, its wet green jaws more than ready to take everything that the Nazis could dump—bottomless, voracious.

Back in the hovel, Rockson had to be equally wary of the man he had bested. Foster avoided the Doomsday Warrior like the plague. There was a strange power vacuum now in the concrete hut. Foster 236 had ruled them all with an iron fist, taking what he wanted, but also in his own cruel way he kept order among the savage group. Now, when Rockson was not there, he still ruled, instituting his commands with snarls, demanding this scrap of hidden bread, that shoelace. But when the Doomsday Warrior returned from the swamps at night, there would be an eerie silence when he walked in. Foster 236 did not want him to know he still ruled. He was sure Rockson would kill him. Unless *he* was killed first. The Doomsday Warrior could sense the strange chill, the nervousness in the air when he returned. Each night he went straight to his sleeping square at the far end where he would sit in the near darkness watching the others watching him. Like savage creatures of the wild, they were mere shadows of men, Rock thought with disgust. Mindless, filled only with their own greed, like dogs ripping at one another for what few scraps came their way. But they hadn't been born that way. These were Americans. They had been taken by the Reds and the Nazis, and had their minds slowly eaten away by years of suffering, the constant humiliations and lack of any pride—anything by which one could call oneself a man.

On the fifth night, as they glared at him with narrow wolfish eyes, as Foster sat yards away, his hand gripped tightly around the large kitchen knife he carried, waiting until the right moment, the night the man let his guard down and fell into too deep a sleep. Then he would strike. Then all would be as it was before. Suddenly, Rockson jumped up in a rage at the barbarians around him. He stood in the middle of the floor, stepping over men, and yelled out to them.

"You are not men. You're animals. You're scum. But not because you are, because you *let* them make you into it. You believe all their goddamned lies, that you are fools, incapable of anything. You let them break your wills as if they were nothing. Look at your goddamned selves won't you! You look like cavemen, faces filled with wounds, teeth falling out. Yet you do nothing. Don't you see, don't all you goddamned fools understand?"

They looked at him in confusion, incomprehension. Their eyes were wide with fear and curiosity. His words, the stranger's words hurt them. Hurt their brains. There was too much down there. They knew somehow he was right—that they had once been different, once been men. And now—now were—what?

Rockson let his body go limp and his head drop in disgust as he looked around and saw eyes of oxen staring back, vacuums into which all fell and nothing registered.

"Ah, the hell with you all," he said, waving his

hands at them. He walked back to his little space, shut his eyes and tried to go to sleep. He knew his senses would warn him of any intruder. And if they wanted to, he was goddamned ready. He fell asleep and once again had the dreams—terrifying dreams filled with darkness and blood and faces he knew so well, yet did not know at all.

He was a child, and everywhere around him was blood. A man lay on the floor in front of him, his body covered with stab wounds. He was dead. And across the room a woman. She was being raped and mauled savagely by a number of men in Russian KGB uniforms. Her face was so familiar. And her screams. God, her screams shook the very marrow of his bones. And he himself was somehow hidden beneath the floor looking up at the scene. Then there was a flash and he was running, running through the snow, through the mountains. He was lost. Just a child without food, water, anything. It was all too much. He sat on a rock and cried as the purple clouds flew far overhead in a swirling kaleidoscope of color.

He awoke, his face streaming with tears. The dream, so painful. He knew it had something to do with his childhood. It was too powerful to just be a fantasy. Again, his unconscious was trying to break through, but couldn't. Something was blocking his memories with the power of a steel wall.

The next day when Rockson arrived at the central

square to be trucked along with the other men of the Corpse Detail, they were instead taken to another part of the Fortress, the troops barracks of the Nazis on the far side of the city. There had been some sort of virus, a mutated Anthrax germ, that the Nazis had been able to stop from destroying the entire fort with a shipment of vaccine from Russia. But nearly 300 troops had died in just 36 hours. Their bodies were already bloating, stretching out in grotesque configurations where they had been brought and stacked in an empty warehouse. Rockson and the others were taken there and given cloths to cover their mouths. They began bringing the corpses out and loading them onto transport trucks to be taken to the swamps. On his third trip out, Rockson looked up and noticed a high steel tower several hundred feet away. He saw someone high atop it, a woman, her hair catching the sun's rays and reflecting them dazzlingly from her long red hair. He felt a sensation, terrible and wonderful at the same time sweep through his body. The woman, she was beautiful. And somehow he felt he knew her. Knew her intimately. She was the most beautiful woman that he had ever seen—not that he could really remember seeing any women. She was dressed in gold gossamer, a fairy-like gown of brilliant reflections, glints from the sun rippling down her gown, her long fiery hair flowing down her shoulders and back like a waterfall of flame. He stared up the distance separating them and saw that she was looking down at him. Her eyes fastened on him and she began yelling something—he could barely hear—she was calling—a name.

A guard suddenly appeared and slammed the side of his rifle into Rockson's ribs.

"What the hell do you think you're doing, scum?" the burly man said. "Load those bodies, or you'll be one of them."

Rock turned around, catching one more glimpse of the mysterious woman, and re-entered the barracks of the dead. When he came out and looked up, dragging a body along the ground, she was gone, disappeared inside the conical steel tower in the sky.

They moved the bodies for hours, filling the truck, taking them around the back of the Nazi fortress, on a long circuitous route to avoid contaminating any other part of the fortress, and then to the swamp where they were dumped to join their rotting comrades in the green dankness. The Anthrax germs had done their dirty work fast, and destroyed the lungs and nervous systems of its victims. When the garbage crew moved the dead Germans, blood spurted out of their mouths and eyes. Every touch of their flesh produced spurts of the still bright red liquid from every orifice of their bodies as the entire internal structure had broken down into ooze.

On their third trip back for more of the disease victims, Rockson saw her again, her impossibly red hair, flowing around her head in the stiff breeze. She seemed to be looking down at him, somehow having perceived his energy directed at her, even though hundreds of feet separated them.

"Who is that?" he whispered to one of the slaves.

"She is the goddess. They worship her in the Hitler Pantheon. The reincarnation of the great goddess Eva Braun," the man said nervously, looking around to see if any guards were near.

"Von Reisling crawls at her feet," the slave continued. "He licks her shoes. So one of the servants there told me. I believe it. They are all perverted down to the very marrow of their black bones. But don't look at her. She is a Nazi goddess. If they even catch you looking—there are worse things than hauling the dead—one can *be* dead." He headed off, dragging the corpse of a young Nazi trooper by a rope tied around the dead man's wrists.

But Rockson couldn't help but look each time he dragged a new corpse out to the transport truck. His eyes were hypnotically fixed on her as if she held the key to his memory, his life. And he felt things—*thoughts* going into his mind. Strange disturbing thoughts, once again, as if something was calling to him. Only these messages were garbled, unclear. It hurt him, hurt his brain. Yet he couldn't stop looking at her, yearning to be near her. It took the entire day to clear the barracks of the bodies and at last the final load was taken to the swamp and dumped in by moonlight, the full white rays of the moon lighting the swamp so that it appeared almost translucent, shimmering with waves of fluorescent energy. Rockson heard the sounds again, this time even louder, from the swamp, as if something was singing dark, guttural songs. He swore that just for a second he saw something, something large move under the surface of the swamp about a hundred yards out. Then nothing.

They were trucked back to the fortress after midnight, missing even their bowls of gruel as the kitchen food-dispensing unit had already gone back to their quarters for the night. Rock didn't even give a damn. He could scarcely think of food, so torn was his mind by all the thoughts that were now screaming around his head like a flock of mad birds, flying, spinning, never settling even for a second. The moment he walked in the door to his dilapidated concrete barracks the stench of the place hit him like a fist. The single candle that was always lit on a small table in the center of the room flickered out a dismal light over the cold concrete floor, filled every square inch by sleeping slaves. They grunted and snored, and tossed and turned, growling and punching out when another's foot or hand got too close to their precious inches of territory. As Rockson walked between them heading toward his spot, he looked down on the rags, the caked faces, filled with sores, the mounds of excrement that sat between them in little piles as they defecated right where they slept. He saw the roaches crawling among them from body to body, eating crumbs and fleks of sour stew from the slaves' very lips, he saw rats darting, scampering among the unconscious bodies, grabbing whatever had fallen to the cold floor.

Suddenly he felt his entire being filled with a revulsion beyond words. That men, his own fellow Americans, should be living in such filth, such stench, that even the lowest animal form on earth would not allow itself to sink to! His brain felt like it was going to explode with accumulated rage. He tried to control himself as he felt an erupting explosion of fury rising in his guts and climbing into his chest. But there was no holding back.

"Nooo!" he screamed out at the top of his lungs,

instantly waking every one in the barracks, the slaves bolted up, their eyes wide with fear.

"Nooo!" Rockson screamed again, his eyes almost brimming with tears.

"You can't live like animals, like this. You are men, goddamn it. You are fucking men. Do you hear me? *Men!* He reached down and lifted the sprawling filth-encrusted creature nearest him and held him in the air with his powerful arms.

With the man aloft, he looked right into his face, which winced in fear. "*Man*, say it," Rockson bellowed into the wretched slave's face. "Say it. I am a fucking man. Say it!"

"I am a—*fucking man*," the man gasped out.

"Then don't live in your own shit," Rockson screamed and threw the slave from him so the terrified creature flew halfway across the floor, crashing over a dozen half-sitting denizens of the horrible barrack.

Now the Doomsday Warrior went half-mad, as if he were under some sort of spell. He rushed among the filthy workers and kicked at them, lifted them, threw them, cursed them, spat at them, raging through the place like a human tornado. Bodies flew left and right slamming into one another, screaming, as the entire slave quarters erupted into bedlam.

A few of them tried to resist as they saw the madman coming at them, his face lit with demonic fury. They pulled knives or pieces of glass, but the mad slave just kicked them from their hands as if they were children's toys and lifted them bodily off the floor, heaving them into hysterically scampering groups.

This went on for 45 seconds, until the entire center of the place had been cleared. The men huddled along the walls, trying to flatten themselves so as to be unnoticed. They all watched as Rockson seemed to calm down, at least slightly. He lifted the candle from the table and held it near his face so they could see him.

"You are pigs. You hear me? All of you are worse than the slimiest animal, the lowest bug that walks the face of this planet. Do you not know what species you are? What have you allowed to be done to yourselves?"

He held the candle to his face.

"*This* is a man. Not a pig, not a worm. You hear me fools? An American citizen. See? I have two eyes, and arms, and a brain. I do not allow rats to run on my body or roaches to kiss my lips, nor do I shit in my own bed and then lie in it. And *you* won't either. Not while I'm here. From now, we live like men, all of us, or leave this place."

They looked at him with terror. They were used to being commanded, humiliated, beaten, but by the Russians or the Nazis, not by another slave. Yet this man had tremendous power; not one of them dared face him. Foster 236 watched from the far end of the room. So the new slave was vying for power. He had known the time would come. Well, one of them had to die. But not right now. He knew he couldn't take on the mad slave one-on-one. He would need stealth; attack when he was defenseless. He felt the solid shaft of the large hammer he had stolen from his factory where he worked. Soon . . . soon. He looked at Joe with a thin smirk of secret knowledge—the man would die.

"Tonight," Rockson screamed, "we start right now to change things. You want a boss, you like to be told what to do, okay. *I'm* the new boss. If you want to try to kill me, go ahead. Be my guest. Now or at any time. One at a time or all at once. But meanwhile you listen to me. You got that?" He screamed out at the grovelling slaves.

"I said do you got that?!" he bellowed so loud that those close by threw their hands over their ears in pain.

"We got that," they answered back, not wanting the madman to start up again, hitting at them.

"Good, now we're getting somewhere," Rockson said, relaxing for a moment, glad to see that he was finally making some headway. A thin smile crossed his hard face. Maybe he could command them into being men, into freedom.

"First we're going to clean this place. You know what this is? Clean?" he asked sarcastically. "No filth, no dust, no shit, no vomit, no spit, no piss, no nothing. Clean."

He glared at them menacingly then added. "*Clean*. Now say it after me."

"*Clean*," they answered in a hesitant chorus.

"Good, excellent," Rockson said, smiling at his unwilling pupils. "Now get your fucking asses out there, fill up those water buckets from the pump and wash this place down. *Now!*" He rushed toward the walls of the barracks where the men stood, forcing them all to run by him and out the door. Within a minute the place was emptied out and just the filth encrusted blankets and bits of clothing the men had left behind in their panic sat there, all covered with so many layers of grease and dirt that they were nearly stiff, objects set into rigor mortis.

Rockson walked outside and saw one of them slowly filling a bucket from one of the four pumps set in the ground. He went over and grabbed three other slaves by the shoulders thrusting them toward the pumps.

"You—you are the pumpers. You keep pumping until I tell you to stop. *You*," he said, pointing to ten men standing in a group nearby. "You men go back inside, bring every bit of clothing, bedding, whatever, out here and wash it down. Nothing goes back inside until it's been washed. Nothing. *You*," he said gruffly, forming a long line of men, pushing them into place one after another. "*You* are the water brigade. When they hand you the buckets you pass them to one another, so that these men here," he grabbed another five of them, "can flood the floor down. Now go."

He stood back as the entire human machine went into operation. Everyone of them would gladly have seen Rockson dead at that moment, but their sheer fear of him made them move, first slowly, and as he glared at them, more quickly.

And it worked. The water was passed, the clothes were brought out, the place was flooded again and again with water and then mopped out two drainage holes on the floor, using pieces of cardboard, turned on their edge.

After the third washing Rock had them stop. He glanced inside. The place looked beautiful. Dilapidated, windowless, but it was clean. Little pools of clear water sparkling from the moon's light stood every feet feet around the wide floor. The smell of shit was gone.

"Now," Rockson said, clapping his fist into his palm. "It's bath time. Whoever wants to sleep inside there tonight is going to take a bath under those pumps. You understand?"

"I ain't taking no damned bath," one particularly dirty piece of humanity said, shuffling from one foot to another. Without a word Rockson walked over to him and slammed the man in the chin with his fist. He crumpled to the ground like a wet leaf.

"Everyone takes a bath," the Doomsday Warrior said, holding his fist up. "One way or another."

He had them line up again, the men in front pushing the water pump for the next. Stripped naked of their clothes, one after another, they went under the cold water and for long minutes were forced to turn and scrub themselves with some stiff brushes Rockson dug up, until there wasn't a trace of slime on them. Then they lined up again on the other side of the doorway holding their still wet clothes and bedding that had been drenched by the wash crew.

It was nearly four in the morning before Rockson allowed them to once again enter the barracks. They quickly found their previously owned territory, creating their own little squares out of coats, cardboard, pieces of wood, and then they all lay back, sopping in their wet clothes. Rockson made his way over to his corner where he made a small bed for himself from his field jacket.

"These are the new rules," Rockson said, addressing them in the dark. He could see the hundreds of eyes, peering back, shining in the moonlight like little silver daggers, every one of whom he knew wanted to kill him.

"We don't shit or spit in here anymore. That's all done in pits at least 50 feet upwind of here. We'll dig holes tomorrow. We'll have a thorough cleaning of the place, the inhabitants and their clothing, once a week. All bugs and rodents are to be killed the moment they are spotted. Once again, you are welcome to try and kill me. If you do—the rules, I would imagine, will no longer apply. Until then, they *do* apply." Rockson let his head drop back and prepared to sleep.

"This is all great," a voice spoke up nervously from the far corner of the room as the rest of the slaves sucked in their breath, anxious that the madman would get going again, just when they had been allowed back in their beds. "But, while you're making us men, what the hell do we do with it? We're all lost here. None of us will even be alive in a few months. Why? *Why?"*

Rockson sat up. The man sounded more intelligent than the others. Almost civilized.

"Who is that speaking?" the Doomsday Warrior asked through the moon slivered darkness, the rays dropping down in solid white shafts of light, like burning pins into a voodoo doll."

"I am Tony-57," the voice said nervously, then added with a stronger voice. "Real name is John Lyons."

"Well Mister Lyons," Rockson said, lying back down into a comfortable position as he spoke, his tired eyes closed. "We do it because we *are* men.

Because, whether we live or die, we must do it as men. When you let the invader take your mind and soul, then he has won. When he has *only* your body, he has a fire that may explode on him at any moment. Because I am a man, I know that inside of you, all of you, is a man also. Frightened, terrified, lost in pain and madness. Still, I know it's there, and as a brother American I can't stand by and let you live like this."

"We'll all die," another voice yelled out.

"Better to *not* know we are men," a second voice answered.

"Only Ted Rockson could save us," a man near the Doomsday Warrior spat out like a bullet.

"Rockson?" Rock asked curiously. The name sent a shiver up his spine. "Who is Ted Rockson?"

The man sat up and spoke in a loud whisper as the others grew silent. Every one of them knew the legendary name. Only Rockson himself did not.

"Rockson is the one man the Russians, and the Nazis, fear," the man said with some pride as if sharing in the Doomsday Warrior's strength just by speaking of him. "He is a Freefighter and has done incredible damage to their armies. He's the most wanted man in America. The Russians have his name and picture, only no one really knows for sure what he looks like, anyway. They have his description up in every military base in the country. Reward of 100,000 rubles for any man, Red or slave, who finds him and turns him in. *He* could save us," the man said almost prayerfully, as he looked out the window through narrow tearful eyes at the burning moon above. "He's the only one who could. There are stories that he has even freed slaves and prisoners in many fortresses. But no one knows for sure. The Russians don't speak of him. So it is all just told from stranger to stranger. But I know he is real," the man went on, growing more and more quiet as the others listened attentively, their minds somehow more awakened by the events of the evening than they had been for a long, long time.

"I know he exists. And I know he will never come here, to this camp, to save us. Not *here*. We are the lost, the forgotten. The unknown dead."

Chapter Eleven

She was kissing him. She was all over him, her naked long-limbed body squirming hard against his as she frantically sought for his manhood. Then he was in her. Her face was so familiar as he looked down at her ecstatic beauty. How incredible she looked, like a goddess. He stroked into her harder and harder. He searched for her name. What was her name? Damnit, why couldn't he remember?

Suddenly voices were calling to him from everywhere. Her voice, multiplied 1,000 times. Her mouth opened again and again, calling his name. Calling his name. Her lips formed the words, but somehow no matter how close they came he couldn't make out what they were saying. Then a chorus of sensations shot through his entire body. *They* were talking to him. Their melodic voices, like a thousand minds telepathing at once, somehow linked into one pulsing harmonious being, spoke to him. Tried to reach him.

He knew them, they were—*The Glowers*. Their name, he *knew* their name. They reached for his mind, sending out their telepathic signals from far off . . .

Arise. Arise, now. Danger, danger is all around you . . ."

He felt a burning pain rip through his head and neck. The sensation was unbearable, as if his entire spinal cord was being severed. He opened his eyes. He had been sleeping, someone was above him. A *weapon*, a *hammer.* It descended with the swiftness of a guillotine for its second strike. But Rockson, even with the racking pain in his upper neck from the hammer's first blow, was still alive—and fast. He rolled his body over, suddenly shifting his hips so that he snapped to the side just as the hammer came down. The 15-inch long, three-inch wide, heavy industrial iron-crafting hammer whizzed past its intended victim and into the floor, cracking the concrete into spider-web like fissures around the point of impact.

It was Foster 236, Rock could see as he jumped up from the floor, slamming one hand around his throbbing neck. No blood, but it hurt like hell. The fool must have missed his skull, and hit just on the muscular side of the neck . . . where he could absorb the blow. He was alive anyway. And something else. He suddenly realized—he *knew* who he was. The blow—it had made it all come back! I'm—I'm *the Rockson*. He almost laughed with joy even as the hulking attacker turned with a snarling contemptuous shriek, attacking with the dread hammer cocked treacherously overhead, threatening Rockson's skull.

But Rockson looked at him with his own brand of contempt. To the others the huge Foster 236 looked unstoppable, but Rockson had fought warriors many times stronger and deadlier. And had won every fight.

He waited until Foster was almost upon him, until the ugly scarred face was only inches away, and then he moved. Rockson swung his hips to the side, stepping in on the charging rhino of a man. The hammer swung just past his head, six inches in front of it, as Foster 236 once again cut thin air. Rockson slammed his hand against the shoulder blade of the attacker. At the same instant he kicked the man's right leg out from under him. The huge body slammed forward and straight down to the concrete floor with all its huge momentum behind it. The man had no time to shield himself from the blow. His face ripped into the ground, smashing instantly into a pulp, as if he had just fallen head-first from a six story building. His teeth and nose ground back into the face. The cheekbones followed. The eyes were slapped back into their sockets as the bone containers around them cracked into pieces. The body twitched violently, shaking and jerking around the floor like a beached whale. The other slaves leaped out of the way, pulling their bedding with them. Then, it was still, as the brain's nervous system stopped and the heart and lungs ceased functioning. The bloody dead thing lay in the center of the floor wet with thin stabbing streaks of blood.

Rock stood up to his full height and looked away from the meat slab on the floor. "I am Ted Rockson," he said simply to the workers. "You were saying last night that he would never come to save you. Well *I* have come! I'm going to get you all out of here, every fucking one of you."

They stared at him in disbelief. My God, he must be the Rockson to dispatch Foster so easily. The Rockson had come here for them—then they were worth something. *The Rockson* wouldn't save worthless slime. His presence filled them with a magical sensation, an emotion they hadn't experienced for as long as they had memories—joy. The emotion of joy.

"We're going to fight them—starting right now. An hour or two before dawn—the best time to strike. I need you to help me. In return I'll blow this whole damned dump to hell. You'll live like men from now on."

The slaves looked at him, their minds filled with fear and confusion. Men? They *wanted* to be *men*, but could they?

"I can't promise any of you that you'll live. But are you alive now? You'll be striking a blow for every slave in this world. And if the others in this living hell see you, they'll join in. And with all of us fighting at once, the Nazis will fall."

He raised his heel and slammed it down into the concrete, making an exploding pistol-like sound.

"Yes, I come," the intelligent one who had questioned him the night before, said. He stepped forward. Just a sprout of a man, still in his teens. Yet Rockson could see by his hard set eyes, his firm jaw, that he was someone to be trusted.

The Doomsday Warrior reached over and rested his hand on the teen's shoulder for a second. "By the authority vested in me as Commanding Officer of the United States Free Fighting Army, I appoint you lieutenant—what's your name again? Your *real* name?" Rockson asked with a grin.

"Lyons, sir. John Lyons."

"Lieutenant Lyons. You'll help me whip things in order."

"Yes sir," Lyons said, raising his hand in an awkward salute in Russian, not American style, as the Reds were the only people he had ever seen saluting.

"I guess I'll come too," another man spoke out. "My brain was dead, Mister Rockson. What you did to us last night, said to us. You woke me up. I don't care if I die—I've been dead for the last seven years. I—I was a farmer before that," he said, his eyes misting over for a second. Then he looked up with a fierceness in his eyes. "I'd like to have a chance to die fighting against these bastards. I'd like that a lot."

He walked over and joined Rock and Lyons. Something was changing about them all now. It was almost as if the Rockson had made them see something about themselves. And once seen, it couldn't be forgotten. He had offered them a road they had to travel now. The road toward *being men*. Another and then another stepped forward until within a minute 75 of the 150 man barracks had come over.

The rest, their minds still set in the ways of the rodent, the ways of the animal living in its own filth, stared with fear and loathing at the group across the way. Slaves were not supposed to rebel. Let there be no trouble. *We will be fed, we have a place to sleep*, they thought.

Rockson led his group out, telling them to crouch low so as not to be spotted. They headed down one of the darker side streets rather than down the main truck thoroughfare through the middle of the slave sector. They managed to avoid guards for about two blocks. Then they rounded a corner and saw a German machine-gun post. Two of the three inside the sandbag enclosure were asleep. The third, nearly asleep himself as he read a German propaganda magazine.

Rockson motioned his mini-army of newly freed slaves to follow behind him, cautioning them to keep silent. They tried to carry out his whispered orders as he tried to get them to fan out and creep up on the objective. But they hadn't moved like men for so long, it was difficult to remember the motions, and they were clumsy in their unpracticed deployment.

Rock crept right up to the reading German and rose up behind him. He grabbed over the sandbags at the helmet strap and pulled hard to the right at the same second his other hand slammed into the spinning face with a fist made of human steel. The man's nose pancaked in and his eyes rolled up like egg whites. Rock jumped into the enclosure and slowly lowered the still breathing body to the ground as the team he had gathered around him dove on top of the other two, making quick if somewhat messy work of them.

They headed on as Rock searched for the balcony-ringed tower where he had seen Rona. *That* was her name. *Rona!* Beautiful Rona. He knew everything. Who he was, who she as. Where they were and what had happened. That last shell from the tank. It had just taken him right out of his head.

"Obviously, *they* weren't aware of who he was, and

had just put him to work with the other slaves!

Mutants luck!

And somehow the Nazis had gotten hold of Rona too. There was no time for subtlety. They'd just have to smash their way in and rescue Rona, then get the hell out of there.

He saw it, the tower, rising bizarrely above the other squat utilitarian cement buildings, ten stories into the air. There were guards at the entrance, but just a few. The Nazis were overconfident. They couldn't imagine these humble slaves rebelling. So much the better. Again the rag-tag force swept forward, the slaves' hearts starting to come alive as they felt their own power, their ability to destroy those who had destroyed them. They came into the five-guard post in a tidal wave of fists and feet, knives and slivers of glass. And within seconds five bloody bodies tumbled to the dusty ground, as dead as if they'd never been born.

Rockson ordered half the men to stay below as the slaves gathered up the weapons of the dead Nazis. Lyons took up a sawed-off Kalasnikov "autofire" in his hands and held it proudly. The others as well grabbed for guns. Men—they were becoming more like men by the second.

Rockson moved up the circular outside stairs of the steel and aluminum tower three steps at a time with the speed of a cat. His neck still hurt like the blazes.

At the fourth floor, he suddenly came upon a seated guard who looked up startled. But Rockson didn't hesitate, continuing forward with his motion, spinning his right leg up and across the low table in front of the German. The heel of his boot caught the Nazi's neck smashing it backward, crushing the man's larynx and vocal cords. The German fell to the floor, gasping for air, his face instantly growing red as an apple. Rockson turned and flew up the stairs.

He hesitated just before the tenth floor, edging around the wall of the entrance room. Just as he expected. Three of them—and these more alert looking than the others. Probably Von Reislings's personal SS unit. The nice thing about being in a hurry is not having to make plans, Rockson thought.

He stood up and walked briskly across the floor with a big smile on his face.

"Jawohl comrades, mein kampf est der Führer's."

The troopers were so taken aback by the fool and his pidgin English that they forgot who and what they were for just a second or two. Enough time for Rockson to walk the thirty feet separating them. As he rushed toward them, they snapped out of their daze and reached for their submachine guns.

But a second or two is the difference between life or death in 2089 A.D. Rockson moved like a streak of lightning, diving right into the midst of them. As he landed, his right foot came up under the groin of the man in front of him, while his fists made contact with two faces. The men dropped to the ground stunned, as the Doomsday Warrior turned in a flash and shot out a kick to the stomach of the fourth who was just raising his sub in a sharp arc. The gun exploded as he fell backward vomiting. Rockson pulled himself out of the way, spinning backward in the opposite direction. The shrieking hail of .9 mm slugs bit into the wall across the room and raced up the side, catching the fifth guard, slicing him right up the center. From his balls up his stomach and chest to the top of his head. A sludge of his innards slopped out like a bloody tidal wave onto the carpeted floor.

He rushed past the sprawled Nazis and through the door they had been guarding. There she was, lying naked on the bed, covered by only the thinnest of silk sheets. Her large breasts were revealed as she sat up, her face grim, expecting the worst. Then she saw his face by the light reflecting in from the outer room.

"Rock—it's *you*, oh God."

She leaped from the bed, letting the sheet fall from her and ran to him wrapping her arms around him, pressing her breasts, her hips, her legs against his live body.

"Oh Rock, I felt your presence from the moment you arrived here and I 'sent-out' like you taught me—but I never received anything back. And when I saw you below, moving the bodies days ago, I saw you look at me, yet you didn't seem to recognize me, and . . ."

She seemed about to burst into tears as she held the man she loved as tightly as a python around a rabbit. The toughest woman in C.C., a fighter who could take on the best of them, her heart melted in the safety and strength of Rockson's arms.

"I know, Rona," Rock said, pulling his head around so they were face to face. "I had a case of amnesia. Complete and total—from the blast. It wasn't until the local bully in my barracks tried to do me in tonight—the bastard hit me with a goddamned hammer—that I came out of it. I suppose I owe him a favor in a way. Well maybe I did him one . . .

Anyway, we've got to get the hell out of here. Some of the other slave workers are with me, they're guarding the front entrance."

"Slaves who will fight? I've never seen that before," Rona said. She rushed back to her closet and slipped into a Nazi work uniform: khaki pants and shirt, and olive-green multi-pocketed commando jacket. Von Reisling had let her order them, having them of course, cleaned and perfumed first. She had ripped the emblems off.

"Well, I don't know if these slaves can fight," Rock said, "but they sure as hell seem willing to try. And that's half the battle."

They headed quickly out the door, Rona delivering a ripping front kick with the toe of her shoe to the one Nazi who seemed like he might be able to try and rise. He quickly joined the others with scarcely a groan. The two Freefighters grabbed subs and pistols from the guards and strapped on ammunition belts.

"It feels good to be packing again Rock," Rona smiled at the Doomsday Warrior as they started back down the long circular stairway.

"No woman should be without one," Rock shot back as they picked up speed.

"Goddamned right," Rona answered, never one not to get the last word, taking two steps at a time behind him, "not when 5,000 Nazis want to worship you like a goddess one minute and rape you the next."

They hit the bottom steps and tore into the street, guns at the ready in their upraised hands. Rock joined the free slaves who seemed somewhat upset: They pointed to the left, barely able to speak, edging back around him as if seeking protection. The Doomsday Warrior turned and looked at the five tanks and 100 German troops advancing on them in a huge column about 150 yards away.

The would-be freedom army looked at him desperately. He was the Rockson, surely he would come up with something.

"What we do?" a voice called from out of the crowd. "What we do?"

For the life of him, Rockson had no answer.

Chapter Twelve

"*This* way," Rona yelled out as the group stood frozen still, like rabbits who await the approach of the wolf. *"Move it!"* She pointed back inside. "There's some kind of tunnel," she said. "I heard Von Reisling mention it once to one of his underlings. He was asking if the basement escape equipment was completed and the man said 'yes'."

Rock directed the free slaves, who had guns taken from the Nazis, to set up a line of fire on the advancing troops. They needed every second they could get. Rock and Rona tore around the main floor of the cylindrical tower searching for the hidden entrance.

"Here it is," Rona cried out as she found a button that made a hidden wood paneled steel door slide open. They went down the stairs and found below the building's electric and microwave power stations. Off to one side was a tunnel, only five feet in diameter, a perfectly round tube covered with a smooth shiny metal. Right at the mouth of the tunnel, which seemed to stretch on forever into the unlit darkness, sat a small tubular vehicle about six feet long. A cockpit sat atop it, which was open.

"Just in case he was ever late for lunch," Rock said as Rona walked over to investigate it. The slaves began pouring down the stairway behind the Freefighters.

"Rockson! Rockson?" Lyons yelled, "they're closing in. Our firepower isn't stopping them anymore. Already six of us are shot. You must come."

"Get the men down here. We'll go through this tunnel here. Blow it up behind us. But fast, man. *Fast.*"

Lyons rushed back up and began herding the men down. Rock could hear the tank shells landing just outside as the damp cement floor below him shook with vibrations.

He turned back to Rona. "Does the thing work? Maybe we could—"

Before he could finish the sentence, Rona, who had been leaning forward on the side of the cigar-shaped shining aluminum/magnesium craft, lost her balance on an oil slick on the floor and fell into the contraption. As if programmed by computer, the curved cockpit dome snapped down into place, instantly sealing her in. The craft seemed to shake and then emitted a high-pitched whirring sound. Rockson saw that it was inching forward down the tunnel and with animal speed he leaped forward. If he could open the cockpit, maybe it would stop. Rona too was struggling to open it.

There didn't appear to be any way. Now the thing took off. Like a snake striking, it settled down and just shot forward into the pitch black perfectly round tunnel. Rockson was knocked by the takeoff from his hold on the cockpit, but as he fell he reached out a hand and grabbed hold of a luggage rack on the very back. He flew behind the screaming, crackling steel cigar, hanging on for dear life.

The cylindrical craft seemed to accelerate every second, borne down the tunnel into which it fit perfectly by some kind of electrical charge which crackled with static around the edges. Rockson reached his other hand forward as well and hung on, gripping the steel shaft at the back with all his strength. The perfectly smooth edges of the tunnel created no friction against his clothes so he slid along effortlessly behind it. But the men back there—the men he had left! He felt torn with confusion. They needed him, yet so did Rona. And if he let go he might smash up and down on the walls like a ping-pong ball at such great speed. He'd have to hold on for now, and wait.

The tube buzzed like a steel bee through its hidden tunnel for about 25 seconds, covering a distance of nearly two miles. They came to a sudden but smooth stop at the other end of the tunnel, which opened into a dimly lit storage room of some kind. Rock jumped down onto the floor and tried to gain his balancc as the ride had made him dizzy. The cockpit clicked and suddenly flew open and Rona emerged with a strange look on her face.

"What just happened?" she asked, "I think I missed something."

"You fell into the Silver Express here," Rock said, raising an eyebrow. "I went to grab you and . . ."

"Rock, all those men—they're . . ."

From far off they could hear the reverberating sounds of explosions echoing down the tube.

"I've got to get back to them. Stay here." The Doomsday Warrior jumped back into the craft and began pushing every button in sight as Rona looked on, not wanting to be left behind. But Rockson couldn't get the craft to budge. Whatever instruction that had been programmed into it had also shut down its functioning systems.

"Damn," Rock said, jumping out again. He slammed his hand against the side of the craft, which gave off a low gong-like sound.

"Let's get the hell out of here," he said angrily. "See where we are."

Rock headed for a door at the far end of what looked like a warehouse, filled with heavy industrial equipment and supplies. He opened it and looked about and gasped. It was the garbage dump where he had worked, or part of it which the slaves had never been allowed to enter. But there on the other side of a gate—the area for dumping corpses, the railroad car and the tracks which led off to the swamps. Suddenly he saw lights bobbing up and down coming down the road that led from the fortress itself. A dozen or more armored vehicles came streaming right toward the warehouse. They knew the other end of the tunnel and had sent men to bite down on whatever came out this end.

Rock's battle strategies had gone awry rather quickly. He had been too anxious, he berated himself, to get to Rona, to see her. He should have thought things out more. Now all those men . . . it gave him a sickening feeling in his guts, a feeling he had never known before—of betrayal. They would have seen him going on the tube. They would think he had fled, a coward. That all his words about becoming *men* were lies. He shook his head in anger. Damn this fucking world. The way it twisted the plans of men.

But there wasn't time to battle a full regiment of Nazi troops, as more and more light filled the road, making a solid line back to the fort. They were after him bad, whoever had organized the slave rebellion *must* be captured.

Rockson ducked his head back inside the warehouse and looked quickly around for anything they could use: a vehicle, a weapon. But just motors, and gear boxes, load reducers, recharged batteries, stood around in no particular order on the floors, and hanging by huge hooks from the walls. He noticed a float, an inflatable device of some kind on a shelf and walked over. A CO_2 raft. He grabbed it and some rope and threw them over his shoulder.

"Come on, Sugar Pie," he said to Rona who stood by the door checking the clip in the lifted German automatic rifle as the bouncing headlights drew closer, a thousand murderous eyes in the dark night.

"Where the hell are we going to go cruising out here?" Rona asked as Rockson pulled her into the darkness of the flat fields ahead.

"Going into the swamps. It's the only place they won't dare follow. We'll hide inside, then come out and somehow get back to those men. I pray some are left."

They rushed through the darkness following the

railroad tracks that Rockson had gotten to know so well in his time here in Goerringrad. They had gone but half the distance when the far dawn began breaking through the thick clouded sky above. The great cumulus mountains took on deep electric purple tones as the sun reflected off their curving mile-high sides. The ground around the fleeing freefighters grew from black to gray and suddenly they could see everything. Could see the flat wet reed fields all around them, the tracks heading off to the foul swamps which lay ahead and behind them. The German attack force was closing in every second as the machine gunners in the lead AMRV opened up with a burst that traced a jagged line just yards away.

"Faster," Rockson yelled. They flew toward the swamps, jumping right and left every second or two. Rock set the pace, with Rona following behind. They had practiced this style of avoidance running in the C.C. as all active Freefighters did and moved along with a perfect cadence, shifting, evading, but never slowing their charging stride.

At last they arrived. The thick green bubbling slime lay at their feet. Rock set the raft down and pulled the release valve on the CO_2 cartridge. "Pray this thing doesn't have a leak," Rock said, "or we've got some *major* problems."

The Germans were within a thousand feet and closing fast. Now a second armored car opened up with a hail of slugs that ripped into a large moss-covered boulder only yards from the two. The raft made a rasping sound and then suddenly was inflated, filling before their eyes in a matter of seconds. Rock picked it up and threw it down right at the green muck's edge.

"Madam," he said, letting his hand drop toward the slightly bobbing rubber craft.

"Are we really going out into this stuff?" she asked, looking quite unhappy about the idea. The rising sun was now a red pearl on the tongue of a far off mountain, illuminating the thick rippling green slime with a ghastly pinkish color. She had never seen anything so uninviting in her entire life.

"Oh Rock," Rona said as she stepped gingerly into the tightly inflated six-foot by four-foot raft. "If I end up drowning in this green mud I'll kill you."

Rockson stepped in and kicked off from the bank. The raft lazily slid out into the thick green porridge, topped with dead leaves and vines fallen from surrounding mutated willows that stood in groups every twenty or thirty yards. "See, I even have a paddle," Rock said, trying to reassure Rona, who sat at the bow staring ahead with horrified eyes at the mist-covered jungle of green muck ahead.

"That really makes me feel better, Rock. I want you to know that," she answered, not turning around for fear that any movement might make the boat tip. Behind them the Germans roared toward the swamp, opening up with everything they had, even a few mini-cannons which sent thick blasts of slime splashing into the air around the raft. The swell rushed under the rocking raft but didn't harm it. Rockson paddled like mad with the small wooden oar, sculling the boat from the back. At first the weight was hard to get going but after a few seconds he made the thing build up a little steam and they sped away from the shore.

Rockson spotted a thick series of groves of the large and thickly leaved swamp trees and headed for them. But the Nazis were closing in just yards from the swamp's edge, pouring down a steady stream now from every damned thing that could spit lead. Rock veered the craft behind the closest grove, getting a little bit of cover. They couldn't afford to have even one slug tear into the raft. The smell of the dank green oily liquid beneath them was nearly overpowering now that they were right out in the middle of it all. Rona kept feeling as if she was about to gag, preparing to lean out and contribute some of her own to the ocean of slime.

Bullets from the Germans rocketed around them, zinging into the trees in the way. The Nazi vehicles screamed to a halt right at the swamp's edge. All but two, that is, which misjudged the amount of solid land left and flew right into the stuff. They instantly stuck in door high as the green liquid rose around them. The Nazis were preoccupied for a few seconds and Rockson took the opportunity to shoot forward in the open toward a second, much thicker grove of trees. He was just yards away when one of the officers looked up and directed fire. But it was too late. The raft whipped behind the high cover as tracers screamed vainly into the bubbles behind them. The mist closed around them.

"Damn. Damn you!" Von Reisling screamed, raising his fist at the departing prisoners. Just feet from the shore, two of his vehicles and nine of his best men were being sucked under to horrible deaths. Suddenly they were gone, straight down into the seemingly bottomless swamp.

"Do not think it is over," Von Reisling screamed in broken English into the swamp which was now misting over with thick curtains of gray steam from the heat of the rising sun. "We will come after you—we will bomb you. You will not humiliate the Fourth Reich. That I promise you."

With that he turned and entered his command car, ordering the others to stay behind and continue firing in the enemies' last known direction for at least an hour. He drove off, back to camp, seething with fury. The man had created an insurrection, nearly a hundred slaves, who had all died or been recaptured. But worse—he had stolen the woman. The woman, *Eva* herself, was gone. He could not believe it! He had had her so close. The goddess herself in his grasp. And now gone. It was an ultimate tragedy. For a nationalistic, history-conscious Nazi like himself, it was tinged with a gothic melancholy. A great man had lost his perfect woman.

With the morning mist rising higher and thicker by the second Rockson took the opportunity to head further back into the swamp, to get even more islands of trees between them and the still-firing Germans. He didn't need to have them get a "lucky" shot in. The Doomsday Warrior slowly paddled forward, Rona sitting up front, calling back directions every few seconds. The main thing was not to get snagged on a branch or sharp rock. There was something about riding an air raft in the center of a vast swamp that made one feel a little unsure about the future. Within minutes there was nothing but thick fog around them tinged with the pungent smell of the rotting swamp. Rockson couldn't even see Rona at the far end of the raft only six feet away. He slowed almost to a crawl.

Behind them the German guns at last came to a stop. It was clear to them that there wasn't a chance in hell of getting the escaped slave. Ammunition was precious. There would be another day. From nearly half-a-mile away Rock could hear the AMRV and jeep engines chug to life and take off.

"We'll just wait for this mist to rise a little," Rock said to Rona who seemed to be adjusting to their swamp ride. Within another 20 minutes, the heat of the pumpkin-orange sun, now risen fully into the eastern sky, burnt off the top layers of fog so that from a distance of three feet above the green swamp the air became clear. The lowest level remained thick with the gray-green smoke swirling above the water all around them. Rock stood up so he could see above it and carefully began paddling toward what he thought was the shore. But after about five minutes of edging ahead, and seeing only more green swamp, more groves of thick-vined swamp trees, and no shore, Rock coughed and came to a stop.

"Do you have something to tell me?" Rona asked, without turning her head, her voice tart with sarcasm.

"Afraid so," Rock said. "I hate to say it . . . but I think we're lost. But I'm sure we can find our way out again. After all these swamps are only . . ."

"Fifty miles wide," Rona said, cutting him off. Something edged through the top few inches of the green slime just inches from the boat, sending a little ripple against them. Rona screamed and jumped back falling on her back into the center of the raft.

Waldenbooks

14 SALE 4883 0516/1 08/24/85

0681335114 5 10 1.99 1.99
082171659X 3 10 2.50 2.50

SUBTOTAL 4.49
MARYLAND 5% TAX .23
TOTAL 4.72
PAYMENT 5.00

CHANGE .28

SO MUCH MORE THAN A BOOKSTORE

08/24/85 15:10

Waldenbooks

14 SALE 4883 0516/1 08/24/85

0681335114	5	1@	1.99	1.99
082171659X	3	1@	2.50	2.50
			SUBTOTAL	4.49
MARYLAND 5% TAX				.23
			TOTAL	4.72
			PAYMENT	5.00
			CHANGE	.28

SO MUCH MORE THAN A BOOKSTORE

08/24/85 15:10

Rock caught her.

"Just a snake Rona, or a frog or something," he said, setting her upright again.

"It's the 'or something' that concerns me," she said, turning and throwing her arms around him once again. "Oh Rock I don't mind dying. Not really. Not if it's with you. I just don't want to have to swallow all that green muck. Couldn't we drown in some nice clear blue water, sink to the bottom, all clean and shiny? Just lie there like statues on display?"

"Hold it woman," Rock said laughing. "We're not quite dead yet. I have no . . ."

His mouth froze in mid-sentence, as she looked at him. It was the voices again, the strange chorus of screams and whispers, grunts and growls that he had heard while dumping bodies days before. This time they were *close*, very close, and they filled his brain, like the roar of a freight train.

"There's something. Something . . ." he whispered.

"I hear it too," she said, her face growing even more pale than her usual ivory tone. "It's some kind of telepathy. Rock, could it be the Glowers?" she asked hopefully.

"No, I'm afraid it's not." Rockson knew the feel of the Glowers' telepathic signals. They were melodic, beautiful, like the music of the universal mind. These voices were broken, brutal. Filled with violence and rage. And they were drawing closer every second.

Suddenly the bubbling slime-filled surface of the swamp for yards all around their small air-filled boat broke into violent foaming and waves which rocked them violently back and forth. Huge shapes broke the surface and rose up surrounding them! Rona screamed, and even Rockson's face blanched. He had seen many ugly things in his time—mutations, creatures that shouldn't have existed. But these were beyond anything he could imagine. They were vaguely humanoid, but nearly ten feet tall, and they seemed to be created from the swamp itself, dripping, green figures of pure rot and decay. Their heads, as large as auto tires, seemed featureless, just big mounds of the dripping slime. Their immense arms reached out, toward the raft, the green rot of their being dripping down from them. Their chests were as wide across as the raft itself. They must have possessed enormous strength as they surrounded the raft, effortlessly gliding through the thick mud. They seemed like living trees made of foul mud and excrement. The creatures dripped their own substance back into the swamp, green dankness falling from their faces, arms, sides, dripping down like little waterfalls of decay. But they didn't seem to lose shape, Rock thought. His logical mind watched, trying to understand them, trying not to be frightened. All things had minds, ways of behaving. If he could communicate with them. But there wasn't much time, for they were converging on the raft, their swampy hands reaching, reaching . . .

Chapter Thirteen

"Stop!" The Doomsday Warrior screamed out with all his telepathic powers, his eyes tightly shut, his entire brain focusing on the command.

The dripping piles of filth stopped dead in their tracks, frozen in confusion. None had been able to speak with them before.

"Stop," Rock sent out again, keeping his eyes closed so as not to let any trace of fear of such hideous creatures fill his thoughts. For he knew that the outer appearance of creatures in the new America was no indication of anything. The most beautiful of nature's creations could kill you in a second, while the ugliest, like the turned inside-out Glowers, could be the most loyal, even *loving* beings. It was the mind, the heart that mattered, and Rockson desperately tried to reach these monstrosities, tried to bridge the gap between human and . . .

"*What dares talk?*" a voice asked, filling Rock's head.

"A man," Rock sent back, suddenly feeling an

electric hope that he could win them over. "A man who flees the German and Russian armies. Armies that kill. We come in peace. I speak to you as a brother of the earth."

"*Brother?*" the voice telepathed back with what Rockson could sense had a certain amount of sarcasm. *"We are brothers to no one. We are Narga—the undying ones. We kill all who come here. We are created out of death, out of mold and rot. And this we give back to the world of the living. All living things that come to this green hell must die."*

The Narga started forward again.

"*Stop!*" Rockson commanded again, sending out such a bolt of mental energy that the swamp creatures pulled back this time with a start. The puny human creature had actually caused them pain. They had never known pain before.

"How can you talk with us?" The question slammed into his head. *"You are a human thing? The others cannot speak with us."*

"I am not human," Rockson answered. "I am mutant. A new species," Rockson added, hoping that maybe fellow mutants would feel sympathetic to one of their own kind.

"Mutant?" There was almost the sound of laughter in his head for a moment, as if the swamp things found it amusing. *"Welcome to the end of the world mutant, for this is the place where the most hideous of nature's creations are found."*

"*Eat him*," a voice from the many telepathic voices of the creatures rang out, zapping into Rock's head like a knife blade.

"Yes, eat him and the girl. They will be tasty,"

another dark mind added. *"We have not tasted fresh meat for long. Always cold and hard."*

The thoughts of the creatures were filled with sickness, darkness, broken images, blood and death. It was hard for Rockson to even listen. But he had to. Had to feel all that they sent and understand them, and fast.

"*No. Not eat,*" the one Rockson had been telepathing with spoke out with a mental roar. *"I talk with him."*

The speaker was clearly the leader, although the Doomsday Warrior couldn't tell how far his power went. The others seemed restless, they stood around the raft, just inches away and he could feel their deep hunger through the air. Rona sat with her eyes half closed, pulled down as far as she could go into the raft as if like a child she could make the nightmare go away by hiding in a little corner. This was not exactly how she had planned to go, into those huge mouths dripping with green slime.

"Who are you?" Rockson asked, trying to get in a conversation with him. One thing he had learned over his many violent years—things won't eat you while they're talking with you.

"*We are the ugly, the cursed, the damned of God's creatures,*" the voice spoke again. One of the huge swamp things stood right next to the raft looking down at Rockson as the others pulled back a yard or so. So, *this* was the leader. Now at least he knew who he was talking to, although any distinguishing features of the slime-being was pretty much lost on him.

"*This is our world. The mud, the quicksand, the rot. We are the rot, the rot is us. We were created out of the darkness—and all who come here shall join us. Why have you come, puny human. Did you not know the price for entering this foul place?"*

"I came to escape from the Nazis," Rock said, searching through his mind for just the right words. He had no idea what they believed or their loyalties, if any, but now was the time, to say the least. All he needed was a political argument and it would be chow time. "We were captured and made into slaves by them. We fight on the side of America. We are Freefighters. We did not know that this was your world, or we would not have trespassed."

"Yes, the Germans," the voice went on, almost softly, a slow waterfall of green foam dripping continuously down its immense chest and legs. It seemed that it should almost just disintegrate as its physicality kept dripping, but somehow it didn't lose any mass. Perhaps the creatures kept sucking up the swamp itself from below, like a pump, Rock thought, continuously replenishing their substance.

"*We—we were created by the German death makers*," the swamp thing went on, addressing Rockson face to face so that he could suddenly see two red eyes, glowing like dark embers set deep in the green dripping head.

We were slaves who had been used up by them and then discarded in this place of wet hell. Many months ago, perhaps a year, when they first began building the fortress. Our dying flesh mingled with the chemicals and the radioactive poison and germs of the swamp. And somehow we found ourselves coalescing, coming into being, if this can be called being. Then we were reborn, from human into monster.

"This is not life—it is an eternal death. We cannot die, though we wish more than anything to do so. We remember our human selves, our wretched lives serving under the Reds and the Nazis. But now our existence is a million times worse. We and the filth are one, our bodies, our minds, made of nothing but poison and death, melted, rotted, putrescence. We are prisoners here trapped inside these monstrosities. We wish only to be released."

"What—what is your name?" Rockson asked, hesitantly, wanting to make a personal contact with their leader. He had learned long ago in dealing with countless barbarian and savage tribes of men that one must always go for the leader, either to influence him or kill him. The rest would follow.

"*I am Nitrogen Carnivore*," the huge dripping swamp-thing said, some of its foul droppings falling down onto the edge of the raft. Rona pulled back, slowly, trying not to look repulsed so as to offend anyone or anything's sensitivities.

"We are named from the foul elements from which we were created."

"I *am Methane Death*," one of the green creatures said, stepping forward next to the one with which Rock was conversing.

"*I am Monoxide Blood*," another said, joining his swampy compatriots. Rockson sensed their hunger growing as the red eyes swept up and down the two Freefighters' bodies like radar domes hot on the trail of a kill.

"Food. We must eat," one of them sent out.

"Yes, they are warm, warm—Nitrogen. It's been so long since we had hot food. Everything's already a

cancer by the time it gets to us. Only an occasional snack of a hand or an arm. They are big. Enough for us here, if we don't share with the others."

Rockson sensed they were pleading with Nitrogen Carnivore to officially open the dining hour. He decided to play a longshot.

"I'm Ted Rockson," he telepathed out, once again using all his mental power, sending out a burst that burned like streaking fire through the invisible air-waves. *"The Doomsday Warrior."*

Again, they pulled back as the power of his mind seemed to have an awful effect on them, like an electric charge.

"*The Rockson*," he heard them whisper from mind to mind.

"*Yes, I remember*," Nitrogen Carnivore said, standing up to his full ten feet plus of purest rot, little branches and leaves, the bones of a dead animal all were intertwined and stuck in his oozing green swamp body.

"The Rockson. They tried to stop your name from being even spoken in the labor camps. I spent most of my human life in those camps. Yes, we've heard of you. Our greatest curse is that we still have minds, memories that will not die even within our own bodies of death."

The tree-sized leader of the swamp monsters stood back as if really seeing Rockson for the first time.

"*We will not eat these*," he said with a firm air of command. Rockson could hear the others protest with soft telepathic whines of hunger, but they quickly stopped. Whatever Nitrogen's hold over them, they seemed completely obedient to him. Rock filed it away in his brain, marked "Important."

"*You come,*" Nitrogen said. *"We go to our home. Show you to others."*

He reached down a dripping green arm nearly seven feet long and as thick as a log as his rough-shaped appendages that served as hands grabbed hold of a rope at the front end of the raft. Turning around, the immense swamp carnivore began walking off into the dead center of the vast swamp as the others splashed behind. The bizarre group of a dozen Narga and the two Freefighters rushed smoothly through the thick slime, the raft pushing a huge swell of the green oil up and around the sides of the inflated craft. Rona was trying to get even deeper down inside the raft, as if it were possible. Rock put his hand on her shoulder and tried to reassure her.

"I know they're not too pretty," he said, "but I've definitely established contact with the leader. I think we're going to be okay." She tried to put on a brave face.

"I guess, after the Glowers and their slurping organs all over the outside of their bodies, I shouldn't be so quick to judge. But God they *are* ugly. My stomach turns just looking at them."

"Better than us turning in their stomachs," the Doomsday Warrior answered, pulling her against his chest so she could hide herself in the strength of his arms. Men she could fight against, she had faced whole armies without flinching. She had trained in martial arts, every kind of weapon, had sparred with Rockson, and Chen, the martial arts instructor of Century City. She had never flinched. But these strange new races, so many of them nightmarishly hideous. She found it hard to just accept. Rockson seemed able to walk up to the most twisted thing on God's earth, say "hello" and sit down for a game of cards. He had a *way* with monstrosities. But for her, give her a good five-on-one knife fight with KGB Deathsquads over these things . . . anytime!

Rockson watched in fascination as they were pulled ever deeper into the putrid swamp. He knew there was no use trying to figure out where they were going or a way back. The swamp was an endless morass of green and groves of thick trees and swamp vines which dropped down. Thicker and thicker draperies of the dark purple rope-like growths dropped over everything like a net. But the Narga with their immense and fluid bulk just waved their tree-like arms in front of them as they walked and oozed through everything in their way. Rockson could feel them playing almost like children, feeling the extent of their great power.

"*Look, Sulphuric Death. I crash this tree,*" one of the Narga yelled mentally off to Rockson's right. The huge swamp thing rushed ahead a few yards, its big elephant-like legs ripping in and out of the sucking swamp. It headed toward a small island of midnight black dirt with about 30 of the 20- to 30-foot high trees huddled together as if for mutual support and protection from the devouring forces of the swamp. The Narga slammed up onto the grove and right through the center sending the foot-thick hard-bark trees smashing over in an explosion of splintering wood. Within seconds the swamp being rushed back down the other side of the mini-island laughing with audible sounds, like pieces of seaweed being slapped loudly together. It lost its balance just as it hit the green surface of the swamp and fell tumbling face forward into the muck disappearing beneath the surface. The others all opened their dark appendages that passed for mouths and emitted the loud slurping laughs as the fallen Narga arose out of the dankness and joined in.

"Ah, they're *cute,* Rock," Rona said, sitting up next to him. Now that she had seen that they could play, she suddenly felt a deep maternal tenderness spring out from her breast toward the hideous things.

"Why they're nothing but a bunch of overgrown green teddybears," she said.

They traveled for nearly an hour, one section of swamp pretty much like the next until at last a large island appeared, this one nearly a quarter-mile wide ringed with the thick-leaved swamp trees.

"*This our home,*" Nitrogen Carnivore said as he pulled the raft up onto the hard-packed red dirt bank.

"The only place we can go when we wish to be out of the slime."

Rockson and Rona got out of the craft, pulling it a few more feet up onto the island to make sure that it didn't somehow slip back in. They followed the hulking towers of oozing swamp mud in toward the center of the island, Carnivore in the lead. They walked for about a hundred yards, the two Freefighters overjoyed just to have solid footing underground, when they came to a large clearing, obviously created by the Narga, since the trees at the very perimeter were knocked over right in half. Their demolition methods were crude but effective.

There were no houses that Rock could detect, just strange round sculptures of some kind, 20-feet tall and almost as wide. They were red in color, made from the island's dirt which possessed certain clay-like qualities and could be molded when mixed with the swamp slime into permanent shapes. Twelve of the structures stood in a circle facing one another and a group of the Narga were in the middle lying flat on their faces looking down at the hard packed ground. They were chanting and slamming their green swamp legs and arms against the ground as if striking it repeatedly. They sang and yelled out choruses that Rock could hear both telepathically and audibly as the watery squishing sounds issued forth from the dark openings that were their mouths, undulating and rippling rivers of mud disappearing inside.

Carnivore stopped Rockson and Rona outside the circular hemispheres as other of the swamp creatures who had been engaged in the incomprehensible activities around the clearing came forward to look at the two humans in amazement. Not that they hadn't seen such creatures before, but only dead, or quickly made dead, and eaten.

"What, what are they doing," Rock asked gingerly, remembering Dr. Shecter's admonitions about questioning native superstitions and religious activities too closely. "The one thing the savage mind can't bear is that which it perceives as any sort of attack upon its mythical or magical systems. Rule-of-thumb Rock: you can eat the bread, fuck the chief's daughter, but *don't* mess with the gods."

Still, Nitrogen seemed willing enough to talk about it. In fact, Rockson began to sense a desperate urgency in the creature to make contact with another mind, something outside the largely bestial members of the Narga. He felt a pleasure in the telepathic signals from Nitrogen which now came in softer tones, more conversational than the initial violent blasts he had first received.

"They are calling out to the Megapoison—that being which created us all—we Narga—out of the slime, out of death, out of that which should have stayed dead. We, I, my people, Rockson, we do not wish to live. For us life is—it's hard to convey to you who are still human—but life is not worth living. Those of us who still have minds are trapped inside this foul wretched prison where all we touch, taste, smell and breathe is rot, disease, excrement. The rest have no minds anymore. I and two others control them like a man would control a dog. But when I first found myself coming into consciousness from out of death Rockson, I thought I had fallen into Hell. And I had. Every minute, every day I have been here I have wished for death. We all do. But we can't die, Ted Rockson. We are already made of that which death turns to, a soup of brains and crumbled bone, a stew of blood and disintegrating flesh. We cannot die. We are . . ."

The creature's voice almost seemed to stumble on the thought, as if it was too much to bear.

". . . immortal. That is why we pray, why they are praying now. To the Megapoison, whose twelve molecules of ultimate poison are represented by the twelve

globes we have built. They chant and they sing Rockson. And they say, please let us die, oh Megapoison.

"We beg you to give us the paradise of nonexistence. Take us from this land of moist horror and into dryness and death."

Rockson felt a deep sympathy surge out of his heart for the band of wretched creatures. They had been cheated twice. First given lives of degradation and pain to live out as mortal men, and then having to do it all over again as hideous swamp creatures. They hadn't been given the chance that nature affords to all men no matter how terrible their circumstances: To sink into that sweet oblivion from which nothing returns. Cheated of death itself.

Chapter Fourteen

Nearly 800 Nazi troops under the command of Major Heimlich moved into the swamps-of-no-return outside Goerringrad in search of Rockson and the missing goddess, Eva Braun. Von Reisling's orders had been clear and succinct—not a man should emerge from those hellish bogs unless they had the two Americans in tow. Otherwise they would wish they had stayed.

The troops had to leave all their heavy equipment behind, as the footing, even using the webbed footgear that stopped the Germans from sinking more than a foot or two into the slime, was treacherous. They came in from the north and west to flush out the escaped Americans and capture them at any cost. All the units would meet in the center—a center that was always covered by heavy mists, where even the pilots of the helicopters hovering above the grim-faced Nazi infantry were not eager to fly. There had been rumors of cannibals and worse.

Major Heimlich was determined that if anyone was

to be eaten it wouldn't be him. He wore protective lightweight body armor unlike his troops, and he carried a rapid-fire, gas ejection stengun. No, he wouldn't die—not him. Not after all he'd been through.

His foot stuck in the glue-like wet green mud for the hundredth time and he wrestled it out, pulling with all his strength with a disgusted look on his face. Hell was for the infantry, while the flyboys just hovered overhead ready to shoot down fire on anything they spotted below. But the only sounds were the sucking of the troop's boots pulling out of the mud at each step.

"A boat would probably be more useful," Heimlich grunted to himself. Nothing—you couldn't see ten feet in front of you. But the major had the creepy feeling of being watched. He glanced nervously around but could see nothing beyond the endless vines and high green stalks that grew out of the slime.

"Calm down, don't get jittery now," he told himself. But the words didn't help.

Another group of Nazi troops with Lt. Himmler in command, edged along a narrow trail between mangrove trees dripping with moisture and covered with parasitic orange blossoms that smelled like fresh sewerage. The hum of the choppers overhead came and went as his men eyed the deep foliage of rot and decay with increasing fear. Fear—an emotion unknown to these Nazi troops in open battle—in a fight where a man could take a stand—live or die. But here you could just disappear in a quicksand pit, or be snatched away . . .

Occasionally they heard footsteps in the distance—slapping wet sounds paralleling their path. How could anything be walking out here, so deep in the swamp, Lt. Himmler wondered nervously. It sounded like more than one, too. Perhaps some sort of multi-legged animal or—his mouth went dry—some kind of super megapede, like those hideous creatures that had ripped his right-hand man, Kraus, to shreds in their last foray into unknown regions.

He patted his rapid-fire smg. This would take out whatever the hell was out there. Let it come—let them all come. And Gunter was right behind him with the new spit gun—a modified flamethrower that shot out quick blasts of fire like a rifle. The squad moved a cautious step at a time, slowly turning their heads from side to side, trying to see through the ever-thickening mists. There was one thing that started bothering them all though. When they stopped walking, so did the sounds in the swamp around them.

"Just an echo," Himmler explained to his men. "A sound reflection off the mists." But slowly, without any of them noticing, giant green hands ripped out of the fog, pulling stragglers back with them. A quick crunching sound, and nothing. One by one they were taken. Until there was just Himmler left. He felt strange—silence suddenly all around him. He turned. No one. He ran backward for yards, nearly falling over in the muck. Something around his ankle—he couldn't run. It was tightening and pulling him down. "Oh God no," he screamed out in German, the shrill words echoing out into the brownish gray mist. But nothing heard him die—nothing human anyway.

Major Heimlich called a halt. "Count off men, I want to make sure no one's gone and lost his own asshole in one of these quicksand bogs. Boll, Bitsel, Kraus, Meineke, Megele, Braunwitz, Bergen-Belson . . ."

Only two of them answered.

"Well, what about the rest of you?" he shouted into the peasoup fog behind them. There was only silence. He bit his dry lips, and tried again, not wanting to think the unthinkable. "Come on now, this is no time for foolishness. What is the matter. Where are you? Where are you." He was screaming by the time he stopped.

"I don't like this," he muttered under his breath. "Not one bit." He had seen action all over this bloody godforsaken radioactive planet. He had fought the dervishes of the Muabir's fanatical Moslem army of beheaders in the Gobi Desert, he had fought hand to hand with the Kurdish tribesmen in Iran. And he was still alive. And the secret to that being alive was not to panic . . . he knew that . . . but the mist . . . the sound of those huge feet drawing closer.

There was a sudden slurping noise from behind a grove of black-barked trees. Something was coming and fast. He spun and shot off a full clip of his exploding slugs and the shape crumbled down onto the surface of the swamp just inches from his feet. It was a uniform—one of his own men. Why didn't he say something . . .

Then the commander saw. He didn't say anything because he had no head and the rest of his body had chunks of flesh ripped from it as if a shark had been munching on him. Then he saw it—coming for him from out of the green stalks—looming, reaching for him with its body from hell. He saw its face, its blood red eyes, its open jaw dripping with swamp slime. He screamed as it bit into his shoulder and tore a six-inch section of meat and bone right off him. He fired a clip right into the thing's stomach but it merely made what appeared to be a twisted foaming smile and reached down for him, lifting the Nazi up in a muddy bearhug. This time it took a chunk of meat out of his neck, severing the arteries. A torrent of blood poured out which the swamp monster tried to lick up with dark burning tongue. Somehow it took Heimlich nearly 20 seconds to die. Just enough time to fully experience being eaten alive.

Chapter Fifteen

Nitrogen Carnivore took off the head of the German soldier he was holding in one hand with a single bite. He crunched the fleshy peanut around in his swampy mouth, cracking it, and then swallowed. Something approximating a smile crossed his green mud face.

"Not bad Rockson– you want some?" The immense swamp creature handed the headless body, oozing blood from the stump, toward Rockson, who held up his hands signaling decline of the offer. Rona, sitting near him on a log, turned away and went pale, feeling her own stomach rising inside.

"*These Nazis are the best things I've eaten in months*," Carnivore went on as he chewed off an arm which disappeared down the cauldronous throat, hand last, waving goodbye.

"*Good, good*," agreed the other Narga that sat around the clearing, eating their fill. There were dead Germans everywhere, being eaten, hanging in trees upside down, being cooked over fires and smoked for storage and future eating. Myriad fires burned around the island as the Narga cooked their booty—nearly 300 crack commandos—now just swamp chow.

When they had finished, Nitrogen Carnivore leaned back and lay on his back against a tree, his huge sopping mass squishing halfway around the lower bark. *"I suppose we owe you that meal, Rockson, since these troops came to get you."*

"My pleasure," Rockson telepathed back, sitting a few feet away. The smell of the sizzling German skin filled the air with the slightly sweet scent of roasting pork, cutting through the constant overpowering stench of the swamp gases that rose bubbling up through the green muck. "And now I have a favor to ask of you," the Doomsday Warrior said.

"What would that be? Your lives? I told you we would return you to shore tomorrow," Nitrogen said, still lying on the ground. A vibration shook his tremendous girth as a burp from the recent meal exited from his cave-like mouth.

"To help us," Rock sent back, brushing away a small swarm of flies that had been drawn to the island by the smell of meat. "I left a lot of men back there—men like yourself—like you used to be, anyway. Slaves, beaten and destroyed by the Nazis until they're consumed and turned into lifeless shells. You know the story better than I do. *They* helped me back there and I promised them I would return. With your help and the help of your people, we could wipe out the German base completely. Even from your lives of eternal pain you could reach out and help the living—help them to avoid becoming like you.

"Ah, you don't know, Rockson. These creatures around me—they don't think like men. You and I—we are civilized—at least our minds are. But they—and even the other leaders—I don't think they would."

"Would *you*? Would *you* help?" Rock asked.

There was a pause while Nitrogen seemed to think about the concept. Then he answered with a firm, *"Yes. I'll help, Rockson. Revenge—yes I could use some revenge. My soul is twisted, inside are forces that want to destroy, to kill everything. It is hard to control. Perhaps by at least directing it against the right enemy my people and our dark natures and energies can be focused on a good cause. Yes I will help—but the others I don't know."*

The entire island was filled with the hulking green monstrosities lying around exhausted from their feast. *They hadn't eaten this much since the munitions explosion three months earlier—that had given them nearly 200 bodies to eat—but those had already been torn and broken—the best parts missing. These—these were so fresh so sweet—like freshly plucked fruit.* Their huge burning pumpkin-red eyes closed in sleepy satisfaction. They rested for an hour or so and then rose and walked over to the Megapoison Shrine for their nightly rituals. They lay down on their faces and stomachs and began chewing on the dirt, asking their gods to return them to that state, back into the soil from which all things had sprung.

From across the clearing, where Rockson sat, his arm around a sleeping Rona, he watched, and tried to understand the telepathic songs, the choruses, the questions and answers of their religious ceremony that shot like a thunderstorm through his mind. Rock could dimly pick up the thoughts of helping him, of fighting the Germans. A debate seemed to rage between groups of them, filling the others with bellows and roars. But at last the ceremony came to a close, the Narga ceased their wailing and rose from the ground. Nitrogen Carnivore walked over to the Doomsday Warrior.

"We'll go. I can't tell you they want to do it for the good of mankind—but because they've grown to like the taste of fresh Germans. Besides maybe—if we're lucky—some of us will die. That is our greatest dream, Rockson—to be given the gift of eternal death. Perhaps for me this time." There was a note of infinite sadness in the swamp creature's thoughts. Then the hoot of an owl silohuetted against the corpse-colored moon.

They came ashore like an army from out of the darkest nightmare, nearly a hundred of the swamp creatures, dripping foul exudations as they stepped onto the ground. Rockson and Rona jumped up from the raft that Nitrogen Carnivore had pulled and for the first time Rona let her stomach relax. Somehow she had thought she was never going to see land again.

"*Which way Rockson?*" Carnivore asked, as the elephant-sized creatures spread out in a long line, their hunger already growing for more of the tasty creatures they had eaten yesterday.

"Straight through that fence there," Rock said, pointing to a dumpsite a mile off, "and then into the fort. I don't think with a backup team like you guys we really need much of a plan. Please, you have instructed your men not to eat the slaves—only the Germans."

"Of course Rockson," the green slime thing answered back, towering over the Freefighter who stood several yards away. *"We are monsters but we're not savages. Besides Germans are tastier—and fatter."*

Rock walked ahead of the field full of moving slime things, he and Rona having to doubletime it to keep up with the huge step of the Nagras' legs. He felt a deep satisfaction that he was returning to help the slaves. That they would see he hadn't broken his word—that he had returned. He just prayed there were some left to save.

They came to the first gate blocking the garbage collection site and the lead Nagra knocked down the ten-foot high, iron link gate as if it were a twig, bending the six-inch thick steel beams over like rubber. The rest followed behind Rockson as he ran down the two-lane dirt road that led to the fort. The lights of Goerringrad twinkled desperately in the black night ahead.

The five guards on duty at the western entrance to the fort sat around their machine gun emplacement, covered with blankets. It was cold here in America. Too fucking cold. It was one thing to come and fight and carry out the Fuhrer's grand military plan—but they had done nothing but guard this old backyard that led to the swamps, for months. When the hell would something happen. Something they could write home to their girlfriends about—something that would make them proud, make them men. The small crackling fire in their center, around which they all sat, puffed out little clouds of blue smoke as the resins of the half-dried pine they'd thrown on caught and exploded with bullet-like snaps.

"Ach, I am disgusted, Heimmel. I want to fight, I want to feel the shells going off around me, the smell of blood and gunpowder in the air. The blood-red sun of victory rising over my shoulder, as the Fuhrer himself wrote about. The glory of fighting for the Fatherland, heroic Teutonic knights carrying out our sacred mission of world unity and purification." His face suddenly changed from animated and firm to a look of the sheerest horror in the space of a second. His mouth dropped open as his eyes focused on the horrors he was seeing coming up the road. The others turned with a start and caught the same frozen expression as if it was a disease. A disease of terror. What does a man do when an army of dead, hideous giants, made out of the foulest mould and slime is coming to kill him? They sat paralyzed in a frieze of blind terror, their heartspeeds nearly tripling in seconds, their faces draining of blood. They were about to get their wish to die for the Fatherland—but not in a very heroic way.

The things were almost upon them, impossible, nightmarish creatures with reaching dripping arms of sludge, and mouths that opened to consume—bottomless—teeth of black fungus. The five guards somehow snapped out of their trance of doom and swung their Kalashnikovs around, shooting wildly on full auto. The slugs tore right into the first four or five of the Narga and settled in the center of their swamp chests and stomachs, just another addition to the filthy mound. One of the hideous creatures reached into the emplacement and lifted two of the Germans out. He squeezed them both, his hands fitting completely around their chests, squeezed until their chests caved in, and their hearts and lungs were condensed into a bloody putty which sprayed out the men's noses, mouths and eyes. Another Narga picked up two more, slamming one right into his mouth, feet first. The man screamed a sound that cut through the air like a razor as the cavernous mouth chewed him down in four quick bites. Just the head was left at the very edge still screaming—then it too disappeared inside with a quick slurp.

The fifth man leaped from the sandbagged emplacement and ran down the fortress road, his legs pumping like a jackrabbit. But a ten-foot swamp being caught up with him in a flash and ripped the man from the ground, holding the trembling and crying soldier up to its dark red eyes. It let out a wet sound as its mouth opened wide, trying to decide whether to start on the brain or the inner organs. It chose the latter, and clamped down its shark-sized jaws over the man's stomach, sucking in the soupy organs with delight as half the remains dribbled down its green front.

"Come on," Rockson yelled, heading toward the main gate of the fortress. "Just this gate and we're inside. You get rid of the Nazis—I'll get the slaves out. Carnivore," he said, stopping just before the electrified main defense gate, "if I never see you again, thank you. Your name will be known to the descendants of this—someday free America—that you and your people were one of the groups that contributed to our freedom—fought to free others. We are keeping new history records in my city and well, it's not for nothing, I promise you that."

"*My pleasure Rockson*," the immense being answered. It constantly amazed the Doomsday Warrior how something so fearsome, so able to kill with incredible power, so hideous, was possessed with such a civilized mind. A thinker, a poet, trapped inside an ultimate deformity. *"It has been good to know you. I have learned from you. Even in our wretched states—one exists, and knowledge, seeing more, taking in the things around us—there is nothing else. At least for me."*

"I hope you get your wish for peace," Rockson said softly, not wanting to say the word death, as he had grown to like the swamp thing and didn't hanker to the notion of its kicking off.

"It is all in the god Megapoison's hands."

The huge thing turned with astounding grace, considering its mass, and pushed over the gate just by extending an arm. The electric current of the fence arced through Nitrogen Carnivore, sending white sparks whipping around its body, supercharged by all the moisture. It was hardly more than a tickle. The army of green death drove into Fort Goerringrad bent on nothing less than annihilation. They came up to the first few buildings at the edge of the fortress and smashed through the concrete walls as if they were made of paper. The sleeping guards inside woke to find themselves enveloped in steel arms of slime, and then, accompanied by loud crunching noises, they were dead.

The Narga went wild, thrashing their arms, slamming out at everything in sight. They had never been able to use their full strength and let loose with everything they had. They had bottled up all the murderous hatred and twisted madness that lay inside them. And that had added to the festering poison and decay of their souls. But now they could let it all come out. Now they could kill, and kill again.

The Germans didn't know what hit them. Everywhere, the Nagra burst through walls, windows, smashed down gates, grabbing every German they found, ripping out their throats with a single quick bite and then throwing the bodies to the ground, mentally noting where they had left them, for future collection. The barracks of the German officers was left in a sea of blood, which ran out the door and into the street—fingers and eyeballs floating in its rushing streams. Those that didn't die instantly wished they had when they came face to face with one of the creatures and saw what was about to consume them. They backed off with their hands in front of their faces, half mad with fear, reverting to childhood states, crying for their Maters and Paters. But the swamp mutations didn't respond well to tears—except as flavoring—and the Nazis were chewed up, spat out and left for a midnight snack.

The fortress crumbled beneath the onslaught. It was as if a tornado—a hundred tornadoes—were going through it, wrecking, obliterating everything they touched, turning buildings to dust, bodies to blood. In their last seconds of life, the dying Germans prayed to a God they hadn't thought of for years. The Christian God, vestige of the distant past, but which their parents and their parents' parents had still followed. These Germans prayed to a God to whom *they* were the antichrist—and he did not hear them. They had built their own concentration camp—and now they would die in it.

Rockson rushed through the demolished gate and toward the slaves' section of the city. He and Rona had rearmed themselves with the weapons of the first-killed Germans, a submachine gun each, German Lugers and a few potato mashers. They tore ass down the main thoroughfare as the Narga wreaked their hellish destruction all around. A few guards heading toward the sound of the fighting spotted Rock, but Rona's and Rock's subs spoke death and more bodies joined in the festivities. Rock didn't even know what the slaves would do. Most of them were already gone—their brains and hearts little more than withered nonfunctioning organs. But he'd have to try. And so would they. Because they weren't going to have any choice about it.

He tore into the first of the barracks and let loose a volley from his sub which ripped like metal teeth into the soft rotting concrete ceiling.

"Time to go, boys. Name's Ted Rockson, you may or may not have heard of me. But I'm here to free your fucking asses whether you want to or not. You, to put it bluntly, no longer have a master. The Nazis are retiring from the slave business as of tonight. Get out of here. Run, into the hills, the mountains. You're on your own now. It's up to you, live or die—as men or beasts." He turned as the amazed eyes stared up at him speechlessly. Rockson went through every slave barracks from A-G, telling inhabitants the same thing. Not accustomed to thinking for themselves, they milled around in confusion and out into the streets not really wanting to leave the fortress. That is until they saw the first lines of the Narga coming nearer. They trampled each other heading the other way.

Rock grew increasingly nervous as he reached his old barracks. Had they all died, left there in the basement? He jumped into the huge room and again fired the sub. The men, already awake from the fighting, sat up.

"It is him," one of them screamed. "He has returned. See—I told you—The Rockson has returned." He jumped up and rushed over to Rockson, kissing his hand, which the Doomsday Warrior pulled away in disgust.

"You!" He recognized the man as one who had joined him in the ill-fated rebellion. "They didn't kill all of you when I left?"

"No—they needed us too bad. We were whipped and had electric shock to our—but other than the 12 men who died down in the basement and of course Lyons whom they took away—they just sent us back to work."

"And Lyons—what happened to him?" Rockson asked anxiously of the only one in the whole place who seemed really salvagable.

"Oh they took him to the House of Pain. He has been the Screamer this week. For three days now. His are the screams we must work to—that are broadcast all day."

Rock told them all the same thing he had to the others. It was their choice now whether to live or die.

Then he rushed toward the pain center in the central square, the place where uncooperative prisoners were taken for "treatment" or disposal. He turned the corner to the building with his sub by his side, Rona running a step behind, her long red hair tied back with twine, in a thick ponytail, her right hand holding a grenade, pin pulled ready for quick release. The three guards at the front entrance to the cylindrical tower where Rona had spent her time as goddess in residence on the 10th floor didn't have a chance. She released her hardball and the two Freefighters dove to the ground. With a three-second delay, the Germans barely had time to hear the click as the grenade hit the ground and see just what it was that was about to take them out. Then it took them out—a spray of blood, bone and cartilage coated the outer stainless steel curved wall of the tower. The two Free Americans rushed over the dismembered heaps and up the stairs, unleashing a spray from both submachine guns as they came bursting through the door. Two more guards waiting inside took slugs to the face and chest before they even saw their opponents and flew backward, sliding along the well-waxed lobby floor.

"It's on the next floor up," Rona yelled. "I heard the screams at night sometimes myself from down below. Coming right up through the walls and floors, I swear, like ghosts." They shot open the locked door to the second floor and tore in, stepping over the corpse of the man who had been waiting on the other side, his pistol cocked.

They rushed down a hallway of padded rooms, each filled with humans or the remains of those that the S.S. had had their way with. In the seventh small cubicle they found Lyons.

"Oh Jesus," Rona gasped, as she saw the bloody remnants of a human being. But the bashed-in face, the teeth missing, one eye swollen as large as a black egg, smiled up at them.

"You came back. Rockson. They told me, the S.S., that you had betrayed me. That, as miserable as my life was, you had made it even worse and had lied and deserted us all. But I told them no and even in the midst of what they did to me—the knowledge that you were coming—that got me through it. A man needs something to believe in—or else there is nothing."

"I came back," Rock said softly, cradling the barely moving man's head as he cut the cords that bound him to the steel ribbed chair. "I want you to know that I didn't try to escape from the basement when you were all trapped. Rona fell onto the tube car and I jumped on to help her—the thing took off. There was no time—"

Lyons cut him off. "It's okay, Rockson, I believe you."

"We're gonna fix you up now, pal. You're coming with us—Rona and me—back to Century City. I can see a man of your courage and intelligence would be of great use to us there."

"Thanks, Rockson—but I think I'm dying. So why don't you two just—"

"You ain't dying," Rocks said curtly. "Believe me, I've seen more dead men than you could spit at, and *you're* not one of them."

Rock looked him over. No large puncture wounds,

though there were cigarette burns across his chest. Hopefully he had just been tortured and not mortally wounded. The Nazis would have wanted to drag it out.

"Come on, get up, try to walk," Rock said, lifting the gaunt slave to his feet. The man rose and then stumbled but caught hold of Rockson's arm and steadied himself.

"Yes, I think I can—but not too fast."

He held himself stiffly erect. Reborn from being a slave into being a man, at least partially, through Rockson's words, he didn't want to give up his dignity now. He walked shakily down the corridor, his body twitching with exquisite pain but his eyes clear and strong. Rockson pulled out a Luger from his belt and handed it to Lyons, who took it in trembling hands. It seemed symbolic of his emancipation—a material object that marked a metaphysical transition from savage to human.

"From this day forward," Rock said, as they headed down the corridor to the stairs, "you are no longer a slave, Lyons, but a man. And as a man you'll have to kill the enemies of freedom or be killed. Don't hesitate. They won't." Rock looked the newly liberated man square in the eyes. Freedom was one thing, but keeping it for very long—that was another.

They came out onto the main floor corridor and walked smack into nearly a dozen Nazi storm troopers. Standing in front of them, holding the inevitable Luger that Hitler had done so much to popularize, Von Reisling, his face bright red with rage, his one good eye bloodshot and wide as if it were about to burst from its socket. The two groups—adversaries at the opposite ends of the spectrum of good and evil—stood stock still, frozen in a limbo of hesitation, each side facing down the other. Gunfight at the OK Corral, 2089 AD.

"You," Von Reisling said, grinding his teeth together like pieces of crumbling chalk. He stared at Rona. "You—my queen. We gave you the ultimate honor—the perfect archetype of Aryan womanhood—a goddess to be worshipped by every proud soldier of the Fatherland. And you threw it all away."

"You've got to be kidding," Rona laughed out loud, throwing her head back for a second, and slipping a grenade into her hand from a pouch just behind her lower back. She flicked the pin out and got it launch ready. "My fine Fuhrer Uber," Rona said, making the eye signal to Rockson, one of a thousand body codes that the C.C. Freefighters learned as part of their training—signaling attack within seconds—hit the dirt on my movement. "I had no intention of ever being your goddess," Rona went on, continuing to laugh, taking the Nazi's attention away from what was actually going on. "Besides, you're a dickless wonder anyway. No goddess could ever be satisfied with an ugly, effeminate, impotent Nazi pig like you, Von Reisling." She figured one of the adjectives would cause a fuse to blow. And it did. Von Reisling's face grew even brighter, almost the color of his pulsing blood, and she saw his chest inhale to scream out the command to fire. Only he should have screamed it faster. Rona threw the grenade so it slid along the floor like a bowling ball, and twisted around in a flash diving backward flat on the floor. Rockson grabbed Lyons at the instant he saw her arm move and pulled them both backward onto the marble-tiled floor. The three-second timer gave the Nazis just about enough time to look terrified and time to run. Then it went off, sending out a spitting shredder of shrapnel in every direction. Six men fell, gushing blood in jagged deep wounds in their legs and backs. But they had shielded the others from the metal storm, and they began firing back from their prone positions on the floor.

Rona and Rock edged backward along the walls, firing their subs on auto just inches above the floor. The screams from thirty feet away indicated something had received them. Suddenly Rock heard a sound from above and behind them—more S.S. coming down the stairs. They were boxed in, and the firepower was overwhelming. Just when things were starting to look good, Rock thought with disgust. He turned to Rona, who slid backward on her stomach six feet away across the corridor.

"Any more grenades?" Rock asked hopefully, cursing himself for not grabbing a few himself.

"Not a one," she said, "and I can see—as I'm sure you can—that the party's just about over."

"I hate to say it, but—" His words were cut off as a slug tore into Rockson's right shoulder, just missing the bone. He winced and then looked up again, slapping his palm over the wound to see how badly it was bleeding. It wasn't too good, as the hand came back sopping wet. Bullets pinged back and forth along the corridor, just inches above them, ripping pockmarks into the wall. From the stairs above, another hail of fire opened up—coming closer by the second toward the three Americans.

"Oh Rock, I want to die holding you," Rona cried out, and rolled across the hallway floor, slamming into the only man she had ever loved, half pinning him to the wall. Lyons, just feet behind Rockson, looked on in consternation, barely able to comprehend what was going on. Rona glued her lips to Rock's as the Doomsday Warrior half gasped in surprise, a stab of pain going through his shoulder as she pulled him tight, wrapping herself around him like a starfish around an anemone.

Suddenly a roar of thunder blasted through the corridor as the very stone floor beneath them shook violently. There were roars, then screams through the thick sheets of dust that instantly filled the place. Screams of terrifying dimensions reaching notes that sent shivers up Rona's back. Then loud crunching and slurping sounds. From behind them, the same explosion of stone as the walls erupted in a tornado of fragments. The Nazis on the staircase down the corridor from the Freefighters collapsed in a bloody heap as the stair beams unhinged and fell. The Narga crashed in through the walls, their huge swamp bodies slapping along the stone floor as they grabbed every German they could find and decapitated them, swallowing their heads like walnuts.

Rockson and Rona stood up slowly and Lyons remained on the floor, his arms over his head, trying to hide from the horrific sight of the Narga. The Doomsday Warrior sent out a powerful mental blast to make sure they didn't chomp too quickly on one of his appendages.

"This is the Rockson! In the corridor ahead! The

Rockson!" Lyons ran over to Rock's side, standing as close as he could to the Doomsday Warrior as the immense green slime things emerged from the swirling dust of the caved-in walls. They stopped just feet away, four of them, and stared down at the Americans.

"*Should we eat him?*" a voice asked telepathically, poking a huge wet finger at Lyons, who let out a scream that echoed down the collapsed corridor.

"No, he's with me," Rockson said firmly. The swamp creatures turned and headed out in search of more goodies. Rock, Rona and Lyons walked over the headless German bodies that littered the hall and out into the street. The fortress was in ruins—half-eaten corpses lay everywhere, appendages strewn around like a parts shop. Countless fires lapped their licking flames into the air, as explosions rocked the ground every few seconds. Towering funnels of smoke joined together, creating a vast black shroud high over the fortress. The Narga had the destructive powers of an atomic bomb, leaving nothing untouched in their path. The Nazi invasion force, the Fourth Reich, destined to last "ten thousand years," met its violent destiny lost in the slime-coated stomachs of the ugliest creatures God had ever put on the face of the earth.

Chapter Sixteen

The swamp mutations spent nearly two days inside the fortress city of Goerringrad or what was left of it, munching on the leftovers of their deceased enemy. They ate everything, grinding down the very bones that lay in the streets, sucking out the marrow like old dogs. Then they left, heading back to the swamps, to their world of eternal green hell. Behind them not a creature stirred, not even a mouse.

The slaves of the fortress had exited post haste from the burning death camp and run into the hills. It had all happened so fast, the Rockson appearing, and the creatures from hell itself. Now they were on their own, split up into smaller groups, anywhere from four to twenty, trying to clumsily hunt, make fires, keep warm. Over half would die in the next six months, but the other half would live, would be made tough fighters, ready to strike back at those who had forced them into chains.

Rockson, Rona and Lyons made their way slowly through the Rockies back toward Century City, over

150 miles away, moving at night and in the early dawn, and resting during the day in shade, so as to avoid any Russian drones that flew constantly overhead, searching for survivors of the Battle of Forrester—and the location of Century City. Lyons seemed very tired the first two days and Rock didn't want to push him too hard. He had grown to like something in the feisty, humorous nature of the teenager and felt somehow responsible for him. As if releasing him from slavery had made him Rockson's stepson, and Rockson the Father of Freedom. The three of them hit it off, and Lyons, once he saw that he wasn't going to die, left the two Freefighters in stitches with his stories of his early life, traveling with his father who was a salesman selling everything from nails to snake oil, ammunition to corsets, magic spells, love potions, and positive, absolute triple-your-money-back money-making amulets. They had crisscrossed the U.S. twice a year, working their way all the way down to Texas and as far north as Canada, all in a beat-up old horsedrawn wagon.

"The wagon kept going," Lyons told them with a grin. "It was the horses that dropped. Dad used to drive 'em so hard, always claiming they was just lazy sons-of-bitches. 'Ain't nothing lazier than a horse' he used to tell me. 'Man's gotta make em work, earn their oats,' And damned if he wouldn't push them all day and night, just to get to the next town where they'd be having some kind of fair or something, and the damned thing would inevitably drop over like some big old tree hit by lightning, right in the middle of the road. And Dad would jump out and start kicking and screaming at that horse, claiming it was just being lazy. I'd say 'Dad, the damned thing's dead' and he'd say 'No he ain't, just being lazy. Being dead is the laziest trick they got'.

"Saw a lot of this country," Lyons went on, as they traversed a sharp pebbled slope, rising up nearly a thousand feet above them. "Before the Reds caught up that is. Said Dad was a spy 'cause they found binoculars and cameras in the wagon. Shot him right on the spot, right in front of me. Then took me off to the labor camps. And there I've been," he said, looking at Rockson as he jumped over a black needled thornbush. "For nearly five years now," Lyons continued. "Passed from one damned Red fort to another like a piece of cattle till *you* kicked some sense into my goddamned head. Being in those camps, at first you resist, you know. But day after day, they smash you, kick you, piss on you, don't give you food, even water. They make you become a slave, Rock, mold you like clay over and over and over. And then one day your mind is just—gone. You know, I can remember the first few camps I was in—the guards who beat me, the work we did. But after that—it's just a blur, like this mist that hurts to even touch."

"It will come back," Rock said softly. "Being free is perhaps the most painful thing a man can do. It's much easier to stay in a state of perpetual numbness, then you don't have to feel the pain. You become a slug, crawling on the ground, oblivious to the world, to life around you. But when freedom comes, it makes you sick to your stomach because it's so frightening, because all those memories slowly come back, haunting you. But all memories fade, and new ones take their place. Most of the time," he added softly, thinking with a twinge of his father being mutilated, killed, his mother and sisters raped, then killed. That was a memory that would never disappear as long as he lived.

By the third day, they were all enjoying the mountain trek. Lyons seemed completely recovered now, jumping around like a young buck, running circles around Rona and Rockson. He was slowly coming to life, and it warmed both their hearts to see it. Up there in the thick forests of Colorado, it felt as if all the world were all right, a paradise compared to so much of America. Birds, circling above, chirped out their songs. Deer and small game scampered around the woods, hardly afraid of the human since they had seen none in so long. Rock showed Lyons how to track and hunt. That evening as the sun set Rona built a small fire out of kumak tree branches, a new breed of oak that burned with hardly any smoke. The woods in this part of the Rockies were abundant with the sweet smelling species. Rock led the teenager through the woods, showing him how to walk Indian style so as not to make noise, to keep downwind, to spot tracks, droppings. The youth took it all in with great interest.

"There." Rock said with a whisper, pointing to the right. "90 feet. See—it looks just like part of the bushes right? A shadow."

Lyons squinted and then his face lit up. "I see it! Yeah! A deer or something."

"A chameleon deer," Rock said. "Or at least that's what Shecter's zoologist boys call them anyway. They're able to change their color to match any surrounding they're in—in seconds. There, it's moving."

The two men watched as the medium-sized male mountain deer walked from a dark patch to an open space lit up with red streaks from the quickly falling ball of fire 96 million miles away. Instantly, the creature's hide turned a blazing red as if it were just a patch of light from the brilliant sunset.

"Now, sight up on the chest," he said as Lyons swung the Kalashnikov around and imitated Rockson's prone posture.

"Don't try for a head shot—at least not with a rifle like this. The chest, lower part. Now squeeze."

Both men pulled the trigger and their rifles spat twin slugs at the same instant. They entered the chameleon deer's chest just three inches apart and passed through the heart, lodging in the lungs on the other side. The mountain deer looked extremely surprised for about one second as its head jerked straight up in the air. Then it fell flat over on its side, stone cold dead.

They walked over and Rock leaned down to look at the bullet holes.

"Perfect shot my lad," Rockson said proudly, glad that his efforts were paying off. He hadn't been wrong about the kid. He was going to turn out to be a good one. Maybe another Rockson himself. The Doomsday Warrior took out a razor sharp, short bladed bayonet he had snatched from the Nazi camp on the way out and showed Lyons how to butcher the deer, skin it, where the best meat was. Within minutes they had 20 pounds of thick steaks all sliced and piled, and Rockson was wrapping them in the thick leaves of the oak trees, tying the whole package with some of the thin vines that hung down around them.

"There, dinner for . . ." Rockson stopped his sentence in midair as he saw Lyon's face freeze with terror, his eyes focused just behind the Doomsday Warrior. Rock turned, sensing something bad was about to happen. But he didn't know how bad. A grizzly, perhaps 16 feet tall, stood high on its hind legs, sniffing the air with a twitching nose. It looked down at Rockson from what seemed like the sky and without warning, dropped like a missile right on top of him. The Doomsday Warrior had no chance to react, but breathed out and relaxed his body to take the force of the blow. He felt the huge body slam on top of him making him nearly black out, but he held on and reached for the knife he had put back in its sheath. The bear pulled its head up, looking down at him from just feet away, opening its jaws and starting down. All Rock could see was teeth, a tongue as long as an arm, and a dark churning mouth of wetness and digestive fluid.

Suddenly shots rang out, just inches from his ear. Over and over. Rockson felt the huge body above him jerk several times, but the head, with its steam shovel jaws kept coming. He turned his face to the side, twisting over with all his strength as the grizzly's teeth slammed past him and into the ground, as if trying to lift up a whole section of sod.

Rock squirmed violently beneath the ton of deadly carnivore that blanketed him, waiting for that huge head to turn and take a bite. But nothing happened. The head was still, the eyes still open, the tongue hanging out like a red hose. The thing was dead.

"Jesus Christ, Rock. Are you okay? Are you alive?" A voice asked from above, seeing only blood everywhere.

"Yeah, I think so," Rockson answered. "Pull me out and I'll tell you for sure."

Between them they managed to finally roll the dead weight off Rockson and he crawled out to stand up.

"Somehow I think you just saved my ass," he said dryly, and looked back down at the thing. Its entire upper skull had been blasted to bits, the brain sitting in a bloody pool in the lower skull cavity.

"Yeah, I know you said not to go for the head shot," Lyons grinned. "But I figured I was close enough not to miss. I put the muzzle right up to its ear and just emptied the clip. I did good, huh Rockson?" the teen asked, looking for his hero's approval.

"The proof is in the pudding pal," the Doomsday Warrior said, grabbing the steaks he had packed. "And in this case, I'm the pudding."

They travelled for another four days, making good time on some of the less-steep sections of the mountain range. At last Century City was within sight. Somehow Rockson always felt amazed, every time he returned from battle to see it again. And each time, somewhere inside him, he thought it would be the last.

So there was a tinge of sadness mixed in the joy when he came to the twin mountain peaks, the familiar woods. For *this* might be the last time he *would* return.

Chapter Seventeen

In the ornate "Kansas Corn Palace", a palatial building constructed in the 20th Century when the corn and wheat fields of America were the most fertile in the world, the walls were covered with immense flags showing red hammers and sickles crossed over an eagle—the Russian designed "new" flag of the U.S.S.A. Today, the lobbies and auditoriums of the building were filled with dignitaries, military officials and high-level bureaucrats—for today was the "historic" summit meeting between Premier Vassily, Col. Killov of the KGB and President Zhabnov, "president" of the United Socialist States of America. The lesser functionaries zipped about in stubby Cheka sedans, while quiet, sullen men in brown uniforms drank themselves under the table in the local bar wondering if Vassily was indeed under the spell of the blackie, Rahallah, who accompanied him everywhere.

Lawrence, Kansas, had been chosen for its long international class runway, its low level of radiation—and primarily because it was a relatively neutral zone, administered by Soviet trade officials rather than KGB or Red Army.

Zhabnov had been the first to arrive, and after partaking of the luncheon menu, several times over, the jowled nephew of Vassily, who retained his post of president solely because he was stupid enough for the premier to control like a puppet, headed out to the large green and blue-veined marble lobby to await the arrival of the others. He knew his presence at the meeting was largely formal, that Killov and Vassily would make the major decisions, so he felt rather bored with the whole thing before it had even started. Why couldn't he just head upstairs to his bedroom and enjoy the favors of the 14-year-old Siamese twin virgins his sex squads had dug up for him. They had outdone themselves this time, he thought, closing his eyes for a moment, savoring the sweet naked vision in his head. He really must promote that captain whatever-his-name-was who ran the sex unit. Their recent acquisitions had been quite stimulating.

Zhabnov at last heard the bugles blare outside and the huge oak doors opened. In stepped twelve bodyguards, burly men in black leather greatcoats, deathhead symbols made of gold on each wide lapel. Huge bulges showed beneath the coats, suggesting something slightly larger than pistols. Then, turning his head furtively from side to side, as if he expected something to attack him at any second, Killov walked in, in his skin tight black krylon leather pants and field jacket. He hardly looked like he belonged to the world of the living, so emaciated was he, so gaunt and cadaver-like his face and dark, dead-looking eyes.

Zhabnov took in a deep breath as did the others in the immense chandeliered lobby, as Killov's eyes quickly scanned every one of them. When he saw Zhabnov, a shudder ran through his body and a sneer across his lips. He quickly turned away and headed across the marble floor, his bootheels echoing like pistol shots, over to a large banquet table, where he sat down, took out a small flask of liquid and popped four pills in his mouth, swallowing them down with one gulp. Zhabnov squirmed in his chair nervously. He knew Killov hated his guts. Had promised to roast him like a pig when he took over Washington. The president shuddered. Why couldn't things be simple? Why couldn't he just have his girls and tend to his rose garden behind the White House. Life was just so unfair.

Vassily came in next, again, accompanied by a chorus of horns from the Army band outside. He moved silently across the wide shining floor in his wheelchair pushed by the white-tuxedoed, ebony faced Rahallah. If Killov looked like death incarnate, then Vassily looked like death warmed over. His face was spotted with tiny hemorrhages, his countenance stark white, his body slumped like a disintegrating scarecrow under his thick wool blanket. But he was the premier of all the world, wielding more power than any man in the history of the planet. So, the entire room stood as one, even Killov, and gave "The Grandfather" the Red full-fisted salute. Rahallah waved them to sit down, infuriating Killov and Zhabnov, and wheeled Vassily over to the nearly half-foot thick solid oak conference table that stood in the center of the large hall. The two other men of power grudgingly walked over, motioning their guards to stay behind—but not too far, and sat down. The three most powerful men on earth, staring at one another's cool eyes.

The orchestra at the far end of the room began its litany to power as all, except Vassily, stood for the Communist International. "Arise ye prisoners of starvation . . ." When it was over Vassily was the first to speak.

"Gentlemen, gentlemen, so good to see you," the premier said in a firm voice and the slightest of twinkles in his eye. Killov was amazed. His spies had reported Vassily near death with a heart attack. And now . . . He glanced over at Rahallah for a split instant. It was the nigger. He had done it with his voo-doo mumbo-jumbo magic. He *was* a witch. He would have to be burned. Killov made a mental note to have the servant assassinated top priority.

"Pardon me if I don't shake hands," Vassily went on, "but I am old and time is crucial. All formalities, have, by mutual agreement been cut to minimum. Let us get down to business. I have had Rahallah prepare a suggested agenda of three parts which he will give each of you. Rahallah has my fullest confidence, understand. He will—sometimes—speak for me."

The black African placed a small valise on the table, opened it and extracted three sets of papers which he handed out. Killov hissed when he saw the agenda.

"Perhaps we should just let you, Grandfather, and your blackie do all the decision-making here?"

"Not at all, Colonel," Vassily good-naturedly replied. "Please don't take offense. I am merely trying to give a format to our discussions. You may make your own suggestions, amendments, etc."

"And," said Killov quickly, "of course I have a veto. This is not a simple vote on different issues. After all, your nephew sits with you."

"Ah yes, of course—we will *all* have a veto. Everything must be by total majority." And so it went, as Killov challenged every point of the rules for the meeting for nearly an hour. At last they settled on the agenda.

"First," said Killov, summarizing, "All actions of any we three against any of the others must immediately and forever cease. That means," he glared at Zhabnov, "your assassins, my fat friend—"

"Assassins? What assassins?" Zhabnov stuttered.

"The ones I skinned alive," Killov answered with a dagger-like mouth. Zhabnov paled. So that was what had happened to them.

"I haven't sent any assassins," Zhabnov replied. "But I will promise not to send any more. Is that acceptable?"

"Fine, fine," Killov said softly. "And Mr. Premier, might I have your assurances that you do not intend to use either your Imperial Army, your border police or your nephew's regular Red Army forces—or any part of your armed might against the KGB any place in the world, for the duration of this agreement?"

"Gentlemen, of course, we must stop any real or imagined activities against one another," Vassily said with a smile. "Is that not right, nephew?"

Zhabnov weakly expelled some air from his overheated red face and weakly said, "Yes, Grandfather."

Rahallah smiled, his perfect white teeth adding lustre to the room. God, how I hate that blackie, Zhabnov thought. It's indecent to have him here smelling up the place. Killov reached forward, picking up the second page of Vassily's draft.

"So let it be written down in Paragraph 11, page two that we agree to cease our mutual hostilities." Zhabnov grew paranoid every time Rahallah bent to confer with Vassily during the conference. Were they plotting against him too? Were the premier and his Negro—and Killov as well—out to kill him, to re-divide America? Zhabnov's eyes swept the room—perhaps the two of them had arranged an accident for him . . . Just at that moment a servant came in with coffee. Zhabnov refused—it might be poisoned.

After hours of haggling they had at last drafted a document satisfactory to all, and its provisions were read by Rahallah's clear articulate voice. The assembled delegates seated around the hall were aghast at the blackie being allowed the honor of reading the agreement. But who would dare complain?

"The following provisions are agreed to at the Kansas Summit of the triple powers," Rahallah said, standing up at his side of the table. One—All hostilities will cease among the three assignatories to this pact. Any differences of opinion shall, in the future, be negotiated openly between the three. Two—A combined force of Special Penetration Forces," (a euphemism for assassins, the delegates knew) "shall be drawn from the KGB, the Regular Red Army and the Imperial Guard to once-and-for-all get rid of the main destabilizing factor in America—Ted Rockson. Three—A ceasefire shall be effective immediately between the forces of Vassily and Zhabnov on one side and Von Reisling and his new Nazi alliance on the other." The three men repressed looks of ultimate cynicism. Each of them didn't really give a damn what the treaty said. It was all just buying time until Rockson was destroyed. Then civil war would erupt again—and they all knew it. "Four—No atomic weapons of any kind are to be used on American soil without express written permission from Premier Vassily." Killov bristled at this, but he could live without using his favorite weapon, the neutron bomb, of which he had ten stockpiled, for a month or two.

Rahallah finished reading all the provisions of the draft and sat down to tumultuous applause from around the room. In an age of sham, this was perhaps the height to which lies and double dealing could be turned into a celebratory event.

Chapter Eighteen

Rona was the first to scale the top of the ridge and look down on the main eastern entrance to the subterranean world of Century City.

"Oh Rock, no," she said with dismay to the Doomsday Warrior who came right behind her, when she saw what lay over the ridge where Century City should be. Rockson's eyes narrowed with a sharp pain as he saw what had caused her outburst of grief. Carson Mountain, beneath which the Freefighting city had been built, was completely reshaped—much of its pine trees and plantlife burned to ash. Instead of a lofty snow-covered peak in front of them there was just a misshapen double hump of a much lower mountain, at least 300 feet shorter than their previous harboring peak.

"A nuke," Rockson said bitterly as Lyons came up behind them and whistled through his teeth when he saw the damage. Rona sank into Rockson's arms, heartbroken, trembling within his strong arms.

"I can't believe it, I just can't believe it," she said

stunned, over and over again.

"Don't give up hope," the Doomsday Warrior said, gritting his teeth, trying to sound optimistic. "There could be many survivors—C.C. has numerous lower levels, heavily shielded by the iron ore of the mountain. Let's circle around to the other side to one of the emergency entrances. Perhaps the damage isn't as severe there."

They spent nearly an hour and a half circling around the wide mountain until they came to a grove of bent and twisted pines, but at least not burned to ashes. The brunt of the blast had clearly been borne by the opposite slope.

"The entrance—where is it?" Rona said, running forward to what should have been a camouflaged opening. A wall of boulders and rock filled the space, cool air from the lower temperatures within streaming out between the crevices. Rock found a piece of twisted metal on the ground nearby and used it as a makeshift shovel, digging away at the obstruction. Rona and Lyons joined in and the three of them scooped frantically away at the silt and stone from where they remembered the western entrance to be.

After three hours of painstaking, backbreaking work they at last managed to channel out a small entranceway through the bomb-created debris. Rock squeezed through, instantly covered with layers of black clinging silt. After about thirty feet of crawling on his stomach he reached an old iron door—an entrance that hadn't been used for fifty years, sealed with a fist-sized padlock. He pulled out his Turgenev revolver, courtesy of a dead Nazi, and shielding his eyes, fired three slugs into the round steel. It dropped by his hand like a dead bird as the vibrations of the shots sent down a curtain of choking dust over Rockson's head. He pushed with all his weight against the rusted door and after much creaking it swung open, revealing fetid darkness on the other side.

He slid inside, pulling out a flashlight he had fortuitously snatched from Goerringrad before the Narga had done their own version of urban rehabilitation on the Nazi city. He flashed the narrow beam around—a long winding tunnel extended off into the distance, the walls still raw rock, unfinished as the other caverns and corridors of C.C. were. Rona and Lyons squeezed through the opening and joined him, the three of them barely able to fit into the narrow space of the ancient entranceway. The echo of their footsteps on the cave floor was the only sound as they edged cautiously through the passage filled with eerie shadows from Rock's bouncing light.

"Anyone here," the Doomsday Warrior yelled out from time to time. But his cry was followed only by "Heeeerrrree, Heeerreeee" in echoing crescendos that bounced back and forth between the tight walls and died out.

"Are they all dead?" Rona whispered fearfully.

"Don't even think it, Rona," Rockson replied firmly. "This is an old tunnel, hasn't been used for eons. It could well be sealed at the other end. If it is we'll just have to blast our way through that too. Then—only then—will we know for sure."

Rockson's words were quickly borne out as they came to the sealed end of the stone path. Lyons and Rona backed off around a bend as Rockson took the two grenades he had "borrowed" from the Germans and pulled the pins, setting them against another steel door. He flew backward diving to the ground after about thirty feet. The concussion from the blast set his head ringing like a church bell, but when he looked up, the door had been knocked off its bolted frame on one side. They rushed forward and pushed against the thick steel for nearly five minutes, at last creating just enough of an opening to squeeze through.

"Hey, what's that?" Rona said, the moment they were on the other side, inside a dark cavern filled with crates of machine parts. "Someone's shouting. Voices—human voices!"

"Who goes there?" nervous voices rang out through the dust that the grenades had stirred up, some yards away.

"It's us, Rockson and Rona," the Doomsday Warrior yelled out at the top of his lungs, not wanting to get shot down by overzealous guards after all they had been through. From out of the swirling cloud of black soot, five figures emerged, Liberator automatic rifles pointed straight at the filthy Freefighters. Rock recognized the wavy red hair of Shannon, Intelligence Chief Rath's right hand, in a flash.

"Hey don't shoot," the Doomsday Warrior said with a grin. "We've been through hell to get back here. I'm not in the mood for dying."

"Rockson," Shannon said, tearing off her face mask to protect from the grit and dust that hovered in the air. She rushed forward and hugged him, tears streaming down her face, and then turned to Rona, embracing her tightly. From out of the choking grit another figure walked forward, his rifle now pointing down.

"My God, Rockson, you're alive," Rath exclaimed. "We'd given up all hope." The Doomsday Warrior had never been so happy to see the dour faced Intel Chief as he was at this moment. He felt a vibrant love for both of them, felt that he was home again.

"Rath—you're still alive. What the hell happened here? We could see that a nuke was dropped. How many are still alive? Is the city still functioning?" The questions flew one after another from his grime coated lips.

"Easy, easy," Rath said with one of the few smiles Rockson had ever seen him make. "The bomb went off, and thank God it was a low-yield neutron device, about a thousand feet above Carson Mountain. From what we can figure out, it was a fluke. The technicians showed up at the last second here, just when some of Killov's bomber fleet were about to saturate this whole section of the Rockies with N-bombs. The tech's black beam weapons (*See Book #5*) took out five of the bombers and then managed to wing the sixth. But as it crashed the pilot managed to release one of his little death eggs. It could have been worse," Rath said softly, "a lot worse. At least we're still here."

"How many are alive?" Rockson asked nervously.

"We lost nearly half our people," Rath said with obvious anguish. "Of those who are left, perhaps a quarter may or may not survive."

"Dr. Shecter—my team?" Rock asked, nearly stuttering.

"Shecter's alive, but he's laid up for a while from

the wounds he received at the Battle of Forrester Valley. Chen's unhurt, so is McCaughlin. Detroit and Archer are both a little under the weather—radiation sickness I'm afraid. But we're treating everyone with the science teams' deradiation equipment—and it looks good—that's all I know."

"What's the situation of Century City itself?" Rockson asked as Rona and Lyons stood by silently taking it all in.

"Critical!" Rath spat out. "We've been working like hell to shore up the most heavily damaged parts. Sections A through H are completely destroyed—but the rest of the city—though it's not too pretty—is functional. Our main problem right now is that everything's on secondary auxiliary power. The entire city is being run by just three gasoline powered generators. That's why there are no lights anywhere in those lower sections. Our main power units from the thermal generators under Ice Mountain have been damaged. We were just preparing to send a repair team down into the steam tunnels to see what the hell happened. But right now, in all honesty, I don't know what the situation is."

"Well, we're here and ready to do what needs to be done," Rockson said. "Oh by the way, let me introduce the newest Freefighter to join C.C.'s ranks—John Lyons." The teenager stepped forward and shook hands with Shannon and then Rath who looked at him with a somewhat disturbed expression.

"Rock—you know we never allow new men in here unless they've been totally screened, given lie-detector tests, and all the rest of our psychological testing. Now more than ever we can't afford to have any Red agents in here." Lyons bristled at the Intel Chief's words, his entire body stiffening.

"I'll stake my life on this man," Rockson said, putting his arm around the youth's shoulders. "If you knew what he's been through you wouldn't have any questions." Rath looked skeptical but didn't challenge Rockson, but he'd make his own checks, even if they had to be done covertly, to make sure the kid was what he claimed to be.

They walked out of one of the city's lowest levels and up the sloping ramps that led to the living and factory sections. The underground world which Rockson had come to know and love over the last twenty years was now a foreign, eerie place filled with rubble, clogging its underground walkways, lit only by greenish dim emergency lights.

"What the hell happened to both of you, anyway," Rath asked as they moved into the main square of C.C.

"It's a long, long story," Rock said. "Some other time when we can sit around with a few drinks and laugh about it. Right now I'm not in a laughing mood."

Rath stepped over to a figure digging out crates of rifles that had been completely covered with debris and tapped him on the shoulder.

"Hey big guy, I have some people I want you to meet."

"No time, Rath," the man answered without turning. "I'm—" His words stopped in midstream as he saw Rockson's roughhewn face. He tried to speak but only incomprehensible stutterings came from McCaughlin's wide lips. Then the words broke through his emotions.

"I knew it—I knew you weren't dead, Rocky boy. Chen, Detroit—look who's come to pay us a visit." Two other men nearby, half buried in the wreckage stood up and their grim faces instantly brightened into huge smiles.

"Well, as I live and breathe," Detroit gasped, jumping up and slamming his arm around Rock's neck and running his dark fingers through Rona's hair. Chen stood up and walked silently over to his closest friend.

"I hate to say it," the Oriental warrior said softly, "but I thought you'd bought it this time. Detroit kept saying 'No!' but I had a sick feeling in my gut. I couldn't feel your mind out there—anywhere—even in my deepest meditations."

"I didn't have a mind for a while, pal," Rock said cryptically, "maybe that's why." The two men embraced and for the first time ever the Doomsday Warrior saw tears well up in Chen's eyes. The martial arts Master quickly wiped them away, slightly embarrassed pretending that he had gotten something in his eye. Even Rath felt the strong emotions of the moment. For Rockson was more than just a friend and a warrior—he was a living symbol to all of them that the fight for freedom was possible. That all their efforts were not in vain. That men, men like themselves, like Rockson could make a difference even in the worst of circumstances. With Rock's entrance on the scene the entire mood of the place changed. The tears, the blood, the pain was all in the past. Now there was a future again. A future brimming with hope.

Detroit took a look at Rock and Rona and Lyons. "You all need a rest, man. You look like something the dog dragged in."

They went to the decontamination chambers and took off their clothes, undergoing the three-phase cleansing process of shower, sound waves and ultraviolet rays—emerging cleaner than any of them had been for days. Lyons was taken off to be given temporary quarters but Rona would not leave Rock's side. They went to her room, undamaged, and lay down on the bed, bone tired and slept side by side, their arms around one another, for nearly 12 hours.

Refreshed by their first good sleep in a long time, and by their early morning lovemaking, Rona and Rock ate breakfast in the makeshift Century City dining room and then went to see Dr. Shecter. The chief scientist of the city, responsible for much of its advanced machinery and amenities, had been shot in the stomach by German troops near the very end of the Battle of Forrester Valley. The last time Rockson had seen him, the elderly scientist had been bleeding profusely from a stomach wound. Now they found him, remarkably cheerful as he sat up in his bed to greet the returning Freefighters.

"How the hell are you," Shecter said with a broad grin. "We all thought you had ended up inside some large carnivore's stomach. Already preparing a memorial plaque and all that rot."

"Not yet," the Doomsday Warrior replied, standing over the scientist's bed in the hospital section which had been miraculously untouched by the blast that had devastated so much of the city. "Keep the plaque on hold, although I must confess I did come close to being a snack for some rather ugly but, as it turned out, nice fellows."

"Yes, I'll have to hear all about it later," Shecter said, knowing there was little time for small talk in these perilous days. Rock waited for Shecter to say something about his condition, having been informed of the severity of the scientist's wounds by the chief surgeon, Stronson.

"They got me good," Shecter said with a smile. "In fact I think I'm going to put in for some sort of medal for heroism under fire. The bullet apparently didn't do its damage in my stomach other than making me able to eat only gruel for the last few weeks but in coming out the back, it severed my spinal cord. They tell me I'll be confined to a wheelchair the rest of my life. For a younger man, I suppose, a sentence of depression, perhaps suicide. But for me, a man near the end of my days, anyway, it hardly seems to matter." Shecter wiggled his hands. "Besides, I can still use these and my brain—however much is left up there in my declining years."

Rona leaned over and kissed the white haired scientist on the cheek, wanting to show her deep feelings for him. For all the inhabitants of Century City had a place in their hearts for the scientist almost as large as the one they held for Rockson.

"Aw mush," Shecter said, wiping his cheek like a schoolboy kissed by an aunt. "While you two have been out playing around in the countryside we've been busy putting our act together here. Rock, just so no tears come to those mismatched eyes, I want you to know that I've already begun designing power driven legs—hang a damned wheelchair. I didn't see why an ambulatory servo-mechanism can't be manufactured. In fact, maybe it's a good thing that this happened to me. From the ideas I'm already getting, we might be able to do wonders for our wounded men—arm and leg injuries. Should have been shot years ago," he said with a self-deprecating grin.

"Well, legs or not," Rockson said concerned, "we need you. Every man and woman here is praying for your speedy recovery."

"Spare me the histrionics," Shecter said, propping himself up on his pillow with his still surprisingly strong arms. "How's Rath doing as Interim President of C.C.? I must say I don't get along with the man. Better your near-mute friend, that monstrous fellow Archer, was running things as far as I'm concerned. At least he has a heart—a human one at that."

"Rath's not that bad," Rock said, "just a little on the hard boiled side." Both of them had had their disputes, sometimes quite vehement with the Intelligence and Counter-Espionage Chief over the years. For Rath, in charge of all of the city's security forces, wanted control, as much as possible over the comings and goings of the inhabitants, and a say in all new military and scientific planning. While Rock and Shecter visualized an open democratic society, much like the old America—otherwise, as far as both men were concerned, what was the point, what was being saved. But the checks and balances that the different political factions of the city had on one another assured that the underground society did in fact function in a highly democratic manner—perhaps one of the freest societies that had ever existed.

"Actually, he's doing a pretty good job, I have to admit that," Rock added. "He's already preparing a team to investigate the power outage from the thermal generators. Me and my boys along with some of your techs are going to go down there today. Rath dug up some of those suits your team created a few years ago—the heat shielding bulky things—remember? So, with some luck we should have the power on within 24 hours."

"Yes, power," Shecter said, his eyes focusing on the ceiling and his own plans for building the bionic appendages. "Yes, I'll need power—lots of it—to get going on my new schematics. There's much to do, much to—" He began getting agitated and coughed several times, lying back down on the bed.

"Slow down, big fellow," Rock said, patting the gray-haired man on the shoulder. "Don't reap your petri dish before it's cultured," he smiled at Shecter, quoting one of the scientist's favorite aphorisms that he himself used at least five times a day on his science teams.

"Yeah, you're right, Rock," Shecter said, breathing out, trying to make himself relax. "I ain't going nowhere. Just a couple more days and I'll be on my feet. But listen, do me a favor—on the way out could you give a good karate kick or something to that Dr. Stronson so he won't come in here and give me another one of those damned needles in my buttocks."

Chapter Nineteen

There was a tremendous amount to be done to get Century City back into even a semblance of its previous high-tech functioning. At a meeting early that afternoon, Rath explained his main concerns as security director.

"We have strong reasons to believe that the N-bomb attack on the city was purely accidental. We've been lucky for nearly a century down here—this time we weren't. But my gut tells me the Reds know that they caused us damage." Rock and the rest of his team, along with the top civilian and military leaders of Century City were all gathered around the conference room table trying to figure out just how to proceed from their present devastated state. "Now, every one of you keeps coming up to me and saying, *your* sector, *your* department of the city needs top priority. Everyone from Folger in hydroponics to Smithson in baby formula supplies." The gathered brass snickered. "But I'm here to tell you there are in my mind just two immediate concerns. Getting the thermal generators back in working order and getting our security and detection devices functioning again. If the Reds made a move against us now we'd be defenseless, might as well just throw in the towel. *Nothing's* working right now—not our antiaircraft batteries, our radar and sonar early warning systems for intruders or our booby traps around the city's entrances. And everything—I repeat gentlemen—everything is dependent on getting that thermal generator functioning again." He paused to see how his words were going over. Although the brass looked a little skeptical, if out of habit more than anything else, they listened attentively. "Now, in order for Rockson and his team to go down there into the caves, to check out the thermal units and see if anything is blocking the volcanic heat from rising, we're going to have to divert all our emergency power down there." Half the room let out a loud groan as they visualized what little power they had left to operate each of their sectors, being taken away. "Groan, please let's all groan now and get it out of the way. But the fact is, it's going to be pitch black and extremely dangerous down there below Ice Mountain without lights or power going through the auxiliary cables so they can get the damned things started again."

Rockson listened to Rath's words with rapt attention. The man seemed to have risen above his previous hard-edged demeanor. Sometimes it took a great crisis to bring out the best in a person. He had expected to find himself in vehement disagreement with the Intel chief from his first sentence. But instead he agreed with every word. It was logic, pure logic. Nothing could be put back in order without the subterranean power plants.

The debate, as was not uncommon for the vociferously democratic Ruling Council, was loud and tense, but in the end, with Rockson putting his two cents behind Rath's plans, the proposal was voted on and passed. Now, the future of C.C. rested on deeds, not words and it was Rock and his men who would enter the steaming hell below to see if they had a prayer of setting things right again.

Luckily the storage area for the asbestos-lined heat-suits had been in the part of the G-14 area dug out just the day before by the restoration crews. Rockson, Detroit, Archer and Chen, along with five of the city's generator technicians went to the large crate and picked out the least damaged of the somewhat cumbersome silver-white suits. Their ultra-high temperature shielding of asbestos and volcoron, a Shecter plastic alloy, could withstand heat of up to 2000 degrees—but not for very long. They also grabbed some shielded oxygen tanks that could be strapped on the suit's back, if the going got rough due to poisonous gases.

"If we're real lucky, men," Rock told the assembled team, "the breaks won't be down in the volcanic area but near the underground waterfall, Lincoln Falls." Detroit and Chen gave Rockson their usual somewhat cynical looks, knowing that the best laid plans of mice and men inevitably went awry. But they would follow the Doomsday Warrior into hell itself were it necessary. Every one of them had expected to be dead long before this. One more dangerous journey was just par for the course.

McCaughlin, who accompanied them as they gathered their equipment, kept complaining about not coming along, making rather disparaging remarks about Archer's lack of scientific ability—or even literacy. The huge near-mute picked up the meaning of the words if not their exact content and snorted, *"Meeee strooong. Neeeed Aaarrrcher!"*

"That's right, big bear," Rock said slapping McCaughlin on the back. "You're strong too, and literate as hell, but Archer's a goddamned bulldozer—the only kind of bulldozer we can get down those tunnels. You've got to admit you can't toss boulders around with the kind of ease Archer here can. And since I suspect most of the problem down there is rockslides, we're gonna need bulls not finesse."

"Okay, okay you bastards, go and have your little fun without me," McCaughlin said, his rather large bulk poking out from time to time from beneath his dirt-coated sweatshirt. "But I swear if any one of you dies down there, I'm gonna kill him." He headed off to help the digging squads who still had countless tons of rubble to clear from much of the city.

With some trepidation the Rock team minus one and the five electrical technicians headed down the sloping, green-lit tunnel carting their suits and oxygen units in packs slung over their backs. The trip down to the deep caverns was going to be rigorous enough by itself so Rock decided they wouldn't put them on until it was impossible to go on without them. Each man carried small arms, and Chen his usual assortment of star knives and god-knew-what-all beneath his black jumpsuit. The extra weight was regrettable but the Doomsday Warrior, like Rath, had a certain clenched feeling in his guts and he was a man who followed his feelings down to the wire.

At first the going was easy as the main tunnel was wide enough for them to go around portions that had caved in but when they reached the beginning of the smaller tunnel system under Ice Mountain the going got much rougher, until at last the debris from the collapsed cave walls virtually stopped their progress. Rockson pulled out the blueprints of the elaborate tunnel system and searched for an alternate. There were hundreds of passageways, many of them built when the original highway had been constructed nearly 130 years earlier when the original Interstate had been bored beneath Carson Mountain. Tunnels for ventilation, electrical and access to different sections of the two-mile long structure. In addition, nearly 30 other smaller shaftways had been dug out over the last century by the early builders of the Freefighting city. Crews that handled the operation of the thermal generators had always just come through the main shaftway, large enough to drive a car down. But now that was inaccessible due to wreckage from the neutron blast. The blueprints in Rockson's hands gave him an instant headache for so much building had been done, so many additions made, that the map now looked like a maze to test the mental endurance of rats. Not only that but as he scanned the thing closer, holding a small flashlight over it, he saw that many of the passageways had been crossed out, x'ed over with pen years before. God knew which ones were still functional and which had fallen in years before.

Without any particular logic to the map, Rock

decided to trust in instinct. His mutant abilities gave him what had euphemistically been referred to as "Mutant's luck", an uncanny ability to just somehow know the right thing to do—from the gut, not the head. It had rarely failed him. He prayed it wouldn't today. They started down what looked from the print to be the largest of the ancient tunnels and made good time until after about a half mile the damned thing just stopped, a solid granite wall blocking them. Rock glanced back at the nearly faded blueprint, folded it up and put it in his pocket.

"Well, this thing ain't worth a snarlion's tooth," Rock said with disgust to the team. "We'll have to, what they called in the old days, wing it." They backtracked about 200 yards and found a very narrow passageway that at least didn't seem to have been affected by the atomic blast and headed down it at slow descending angle. There were no lights in this part of the subterranean system so the men made their way cautiously along the razor-sharp stalagmite covered ground. After 15 minutes the temperature began rising, a good sign to Rock as it meant they were drawing closer to the dormant volcano that powered the thermal units. The air grew thick and the men began sucking in rasping breaths, beads of sweat covering their faces.

"Suit time," Rock said, stopping. It would make the going a little tougher but the gases released by the volcano were poisonous and undetectable by smell. The men took out the bulky suits and with some difficulty in the narrow tunnel put them on. They walked for another five minutes until they came to an intersection for five different passageways all leading off in different directions.

"Great," Rockson said, as they stopped and gazed off down the pitchblack stone corridors. He was concerned not just about reaching their goal, but about finding their way back.

"Jesus, Rock," Detroit said, "a man could get lost down here for the next thousand years."

"A little pre-planning is always a good idea," Chen spoke out, his voice muffled behind his oxygen mask. "I brought some nylon line, only a hundredth of an inch thick, but we can unravel it, and find our way back later. An old Ninja trick," he said, taking out the spool and tying it around a stalagmite.

"Now, why didn't I think of that?" the Doomsday Warrior said.

"Because you're not an inscrutable Oriental," Chen answered. Rock checked the blueprints again and this time they did show the five intersecting tunnels, two of which appeared to lead to their destination. He looked down both, felt a certain tingling about the one to the right and headed the men in that direction as Chen attached the coil of nylon filament to his waist utility belt and let it unravel. The ceiling of the stone pathway grew lower and lower as they moved on until the men were bending over to avoid bumping their heads. Archer seemed quite uncomfortable as he was almost doubled over and the men could hear what sounded like snarls coming from within his mask. He remembered a rather nasty experience in the subways of Moscow (*See Book #4*) and didn't like cramped underground spaces one bit.

They walked on at a slow pace, careful not to rip their shielding suits on the sharp rock walls. Even the tiniest of tears could mean death, and the temperature gauges on their belts had already risen to 130 degrees. Rock relaxed when he dimly heard the bubbling volcanic roar of the pit, a giant lava dome under Ice Mountain ahead. At last they reached it, suddenly emerging from out of their cramped passage into a large cavern, its jagged ceiling nearly a hundred feet high. And just ahead, the round top of the crater from which clouds of steam rose through crevices to the surface nearly two miles above. The team moved carefully ahead to the nearly 1,200-foot wide pit which glowed with an eerie reddish-orange light from the churning lava miles below. And above the pit, mounted all around it were 20 immense electricity-producing heat generators. Really nothing more than 30-foot long propellers mounted in steel casings, they sat above the rising steam clouds, just reaching out over the volcanic dome and collected the immeasurable amount of energy that was being put out. The steam and the rising air turned the alloy blades with tremendous velocity, causing an electromagnetic generator, placed some 50 feet back from the edge of the dome, to turn out a constant, eternal source of power. So successful were the heat motors, designed by Dr. Shecter nearly 30 years earlier as one of his first, but not last, technologies contributed to Century City, so much power was produced by the generators that only half could even be used. In fact, when everything was functioning, there was a surplus that was stored in cadmium/radion batteries and used for powering mobile equipment. Only now nothing was working. The generators were dead, the windmill-sized blades still as dead branches on a windless day.

Rock hoped it wasn't the blades themselves since they didn't have the equipment for that kind of work. They edged closer nervously as the roar from the sleeping volcano ahead was almost deafening. The heat gauges on their suits went up nearly ten degrees every foot they drew closer to the edge until at 20 feet away the meters read out 230 degrees. Even inside the suits they were starting to sweat.

"What the hell could it be?" Rock asked the head technician Rogers. "All the blades stopping at once like that."

"There's a safety mechanism built into them," Rogers answered yelling above the spiraling clouds of steam ahead, already fogging over their face masks. "Electrically powered. Actually what it does is send them a little zap of electric power every 1/10th of a second. This allows the blades to continue rotating. But if the power stops even once, they'll come to an instant halt. It's a good idea, theoretically anyway."

"So it's that safety that's out?" Rock asked as the rest of the team gathered round to listen.

"Gotta be," Rogers said. "Either the computerized timer or the main cable that feeds into them. And that, I'm afraid, is all the way around the other side of this rather hot barbecue pit. It's easily accessible from the main tunnel—but from here . . ."

There was a narrow walkway around the perimeter of the dome, designed and built years earlier when the heat output of the volcano was a third of its present volume. Rockson looked at the stone steps leading to it through the rising clouds and gulped. It was going to be hot out there. But he didn't know how hot. Leading the way, the Doomsday Warrior stepped up onto the three-foot wide walk and started walking cautiously forward. It was like going into a steambath on the sun. The heat gauges on their belts doubled within seconds as the rest of the repair expedition followed behind, their faces reddening inside their masks, their breath coming in short quick bursts even with the oxygen feed. They could see down through the curtains of steam to a burning glow far below, could feel the raw power of nature course through their bones. And it made them feel like ants—mere nothings compared to the sheer screaming energy that raged beneath their feet. Out of this man had been born, and back into it he would someday go. Each prayed it wouldn't be today.

The going was very slow as the years of rising moisture had deposited a layer of grease on the walk, making it as slippery as wet moss. And those who reached out to grab hold of the iron railing that ran alongside the stone path pulled their hands back in pain as the super-heated metal singed their thick workgloves. But after nearly an hour of slipping and sliding they made it all the way around to the other side and down onto a flat rock plateau filled with heavy machinery and cables running off in every direction. Rogers immediately rushed over to the computerized safety timer and checked it. But after twenty minutes of testing various circuitries he could find nothing wrong.

"It's got to be the main feed," he told Rockson, "over here." He led them to a thickly shielded cable nearly a foot thick that ran out the back of the computer transmitter and followed it toward the volcano searching for breaks. He had gone about forty feet when he stopped in his tracks. "Rock," he said pointing down at the ground, "it's been severed right in half." The cable lay there on the rocky ground, thousands of wires poking out of its dismembered body. Rogers walked to the edge of the volcano and peered down. The other end lay on an outcropping about thirty feet below, with a large boulder resting on top of it.

"Jesus Christ," he muttered as he stared down.

"Can't we just cut off that section and reconnect the other part which looks like it comes back up about fifty feet to the right?" Rogers glanced over to the direction Rockson was pointing to see the other section of cable snaking its way back up onto the plateau.

"No can do Rock," the head tech said grimly. "The thing just reaches itself—no slack. And the electrical supply warehouse back in C.C. is under about a million tons of rock. Won't be dug out for weeks, maybe months. No, I'm afraid," he said, his lips growing even drier, "that we're going to have to go down and get that baby." The men of the Rock Squad and the technicians all stared down into the flaming hell with a sinking sensation in their stomachs.

"First, let's try to just pull the goddamned thing out," Rock said, leading the men to where the cable once again rose out of the pit. "Archer, give it the old one-two." The huge near-mute, wrapped his arms around the cable and pulled back with all his strength. Muscles the size of cantaloupes ballooned up along his massive arms as he strained with every fibre of his being. But nothing happened. The boulder on the downed cable rested as if claiming it as its prey.

"Well," Rock said slowly, "I guess we're going to have to go down there." Every man volunteered at the same instant.

"Thanks guys," the Doomsday Warrior said, "but I'm going to have to pull rank and volunteer myself—and Archer here. His bulldozer abilities may come in handy down there."

"And me," Rogers spoke up. "You're going to have to handle that cable very carefully so as not to destroy the inner wiring, if it isn't already crushed flat. You'll need direction—ergo I'm coming along for the ride."

Rogers went and dragged a portable collapsible magna/steel ladder from a storage shed and lowered it over the side of the dome, attaching its upper support rungs to the iron handrail that ran around the perimeter of the crater. Rockson tested the ladder, yanking it hard, and then went over the side, slowly lowering himself step by rickety step as the ladder swayed back and forth beneath his weight. If it was hot up top, once he actually entered the path of the rising steam and heat it was almost unbearable. He felt as if his body was going to explode, the blood and flesh bubbling right out of him. There was no way they could take more than a few minutes of this.

He reached the ledge, about three yards long by a yard wide upon which rested the torn cable and its guardian boulder. Archer followed next, the ladder groaning and stretching out slightly beneath his massive weight, then Rogers until all three men could barely fit on the outcrop. It was as if they were in the volcano itself, partaking of the mysteries of its primal energies. The lava far below churning like a hurricane of starfire, the heat and steam rose in such force that they could almost reach out and touch its physical presence, and the walls around them vibrated with deep shudders that shook their very bones. Rogers got down on his hands and knees and peered under the two ton boulder, to see just what the damage was. After a few seconds he rose and put his mouth against Rock's ear, screaming over the freight train roar going past them.

"It's better than I'd hoped. The cable was neatly severed—only about six inches of it has been destroyed. The boulder is pointed at the bottom, one edge resting right in a small hole. If we could push it straight out, I think we'll be all right." Archer got around toward the back of the almost egg-shaped 7-foot high boulder while Rock and Rogers went to each side.

"One, two, three," Rock yelled out and they all heaved with every bit of their strength. The boulder seemed to budge perhaps a half an inch and then settled back. They tried again, breathing deeply and then on three, exhaling and pushing to their limit.

Rogers' hand slipped suddenly on the outer edge and he flew forward toward the bubbling hell pit. Rockson saw the motion and in a flash let go of the immense piece of granite and swung his arm out trying to grab the falling technician. Somehow Rogers' hand swung out as he went past and made contact with Rockson's fingers. He hung on the very edge of the precipice, his body hanging out over the fires below held only by three fingers of the Doomsday Warrior's outstretched right hand. But the workglove he wore was meant to be used as a heat shield and protection for the skin below—not as a supporter of 200 pounds plus of weight. Slowly, before both men's horrified eyes, the seams in the wrist part of the glove began giving way inch by nylon-stitched inch. Then it parted—parted the division between life and death. The glove ripped free of Rogers' hand and he fell backward into the murderous smoke and steam.

"Jesus God," Rock muttered inside his mask as he watched the head technician disappear down into the burning depths. He couldn't even hear the screams above the tornado-like roar. "What a fucking way to go," he spat out in disgust. The image of Rogers splashing into the white hot lava sea below came into his head and he quickly pushed it away. There were a lot better ways a man could die.

"Arrrcheer feeeel siiick," the Freefigher giant groaned out to Rockson as he turned back. It was too hot, too damned hot. They'd be dead in minutes. He looked up at Archer who towered above his own 6' 3" frame and spoke with slow firm words.

"We've got to do this, Archer. You understand what I'm saying. You and me—right now—we've got to push this fucker off or it's over. Just think of that old cow you used to carry around from meadow to meadow so it could graze, that you told me about."

"Aarrrchheer uuunderrrsttannd, Roockssn. Bouulder deead." The two Freefighters got around the immense rock and put their legs up against it, both of them getting from behind.

"One, two, three . . ." They both kicked out, slamming into their stone adversary with everything they had. It was like trying to push a mountain, as the thing barely seemed to move. Their muscles tightened into hard balls within their legs, their faces grew redder and redder as if about to burst. But slowly, somehow, impossibly, the boulder began to grudgingly move a fraction of an inch at a time.

"Push, push," Rockson screamed out, knowing they had only one shot to give it their all. Archer reached down into his guts, down into his mountain-man heritage where one is on one's own and only the toughest of the tough survived. With a howl of animal pain he summoned up everything within him and shot it out against the boulder. As if now wanting to itself fall into the pit, the huge weight came to an upright position and hovered like a perfectly balanced sculpture. Rockson gave it his shot too, his veins popping out on his thighs and calves like worms burrowing beneath the skin. But it was enough—just enough. The boulder leaned over, slowly at first, and then with increasing speed toward the steam clouds. It fell from the ledge and plummeted down end over end to join its laval relatives below.

Rock and Archer had to fall on their asses and hold on for dear life on the ledge so as not to go over themselves. Then they rose and Rock checked the cable. It didn't appear to have been further damaged.

"Pull it up," Rock screamed up to the men above, waving his arms in an upward motion so they'd understand. Like a snake rising into a tree, the long cable ascended the pock-marked volcanic wall.

"Let's get the hell out of here, pal," Rock yelled out to Archer who nodded vigorously. They made their way back up the ladder, glad to be back on solid footing. The 300 degrees on the cavern floor seemed like a fall breeze compared to being inside the thing. The four remaining technicians quickly placed the two ends of the split cable together and began rewiring.

"How's it look?" Rock asked, leaning over.

"About an hour," Jenkins, the assistant electrical chief said, making the thumbs up. "Century City will have power by tonight."

Chapter Twenty

Explosions! All around Rockson. The walls suddenly caved in in a screaming avalanche of boulders and rocks. He dove forward with a powerful kick and hit the dirt in the large cave ahead, rolling over and over on his side. He came up in a half-crouch and looked back. The entire tunnel for a distance of about thirty feet had been sealed in by the collapse. The men—they could all be dead. He rose, and walked slowly forward, making sure that no more of the sky was about to fall down. He came up to the wedge of rocks covered with a curtain of dust that completely filled the tunnel he had just been leading his men through.

"Anyone there?" Rockson yelled at the top of his lungs. Nothing. He yelled again. "Anyone there? Archer? Jenkins?"

Suddenly, he heard a far-off muffled sound. He couldn't tell what it was, but something. Something human. He began digging with his bare hands, ripping away at the rock wall and throwing debris to the side. It was insane, he knew. It would take days to clear this. But he had no choice. They could be dying right now. He ripped away at the fallen rocks, some of them as big as his chest. His hands quickly turned bloody, his chest scraped and raw as he pushed with every bit of strength he possessed, ready to kill himself like an old workhorse in the process of doing what he had to.

"Rockson!" Rockson's ears perked up, as he heaved two pineapple-sized chunks of granite off to the side.

"Rockson," again, a voice coming from behind him. But there was no one else with them, unless more C.C. techs had come. He turned and looked back into the large cavern that opened from out of the tunnel. It was dark, hard to see, lit only by an occasional flickering bulb strung up along the wall. He saw a shadowly shape jump suddenly down from an outcropping about 15 feet up on a far wall and start toward him.

"Who the hell is that?" Rock yelled out, growing apprehensive. He reached for his shotgun pistol.

"Your doom, Ted Rockson," the voice said back with icy venom dripping like death itself from those two words. A shiver ran down Rockson's back. This whole thing had been planned—the cave in, but by whom? KGB? Nazis?

He saw the figure emerge from out of the shadows into a streak of hot light. A man, all in black, a Ninja with a mask covering his face. Rockson knew the style instantly just from the ankle to neck costume and the short sword at the side. He had spent years studying the martial arts. Not just application but history and lineage as well. The man looked like the genuine article. He walked forward with a flowing, effortless motion, as he carefully placed each foot ahead of the next, as if stepping on rice paper.

"Look pal, do me a favor," Rock said, lifting his shot pistol up to waist level. "You can't even imagine what I've been through lately. Wars, amnesia, slavery, swamp monsters. Please. Please do me a favor. Just go home to whoever your master is, Killov or Vassily or the Fuhrer himself. But I'm really not in the mood for fighting."

"Don't be ridiculous, Rockson," the voice laughed. "You know you must die—right now. And I will do it."

"Have it your way," the Doomsday Warrior said with a slight twitch of his lower lip, as he pulled the trigger on the shot pistol. The huge gun exploded with a dinosaur-like roar and the x-shaped teflon coated shot roared toward the ninja like an express train looking to crash into flesh. But just as suddenly, where the ninja had stood was only a puff of purple smoke and when it cleared he was gone. Rockson edged back to the sheer rock wall behind him, crouching down, his eyes scanning the large natural cavern back and forth like a hawk. His mind ran through every bit of information he could remember about ninja. How they relied on stealth, smoke, and hidden weaponry to accomplish their ends. He and Chen had worked on countering a number of ninja attack styles, but that had been play. This guy was out to kill him.

Suddenly he remembered—their main attack strategy was to come from the rear, flank their opponent and then . . . Rockson looked up—sheer granite nearly fifty feet in the air with virtually no hand or footholds. He was safe there. Where the hell was the bastard?

Rock saw a sudden glint of something nearly 200 feet across the cave floor and fired with his shot pistol set on tight pattern. But the hot lead just slammed into the wall sending out a veil of dust. The guy was good—real good.

The Doomsday Warrior quickly stripped off the white-thermal protection suit. It was both a blinding bullseye for anyone after him and cumbersome as hell. In his loose civvies his arms and legs were completely free. Now he was ready. Rock chose to stay right where he was—let *him* come after me, that's what he's getting paid for. But even with his super normal powers of perception he just didn't pick up anything. Not a sound, not a blur of movement. Rock searched his mind, trying to remember everything he could about the secret society of killers that had existed for centuries—perhaps the greatest assassins the earth had ever known.

"They thrive on drama," Chen had told him. "Each one trying to create a new, more incredible method of attack, each trying to outdo the other. They kill with a flourish, Rock, getting their pleasure from completely breaching their opponent's defense as if they were paper, humiliating them, before the death blow."

The Doomsday Warrior looked everywhere, tried to use his mutant ESP to feel the man. He sensed his presence but it almost seemed diffuse, the assassin might himself have extra-sensory perceptions and be sending out a psychic smoke screen. Where the hell was he? Tunneling underneath? Impossible! Nothing could go through granite. Not even a laser digger. Above?

He looked up and saw hurtling down dark lightning bolts—two spears, their steel shafts heading straight for his skull. Rockson dove forward in a flash, landing hard on the uneven sharp-edged floor of the cavern as the two shafts ripped into the stone where he had been standing, sending out a shower of yellow sparks. Then they fell harmlessly over on their sides, unbloodied. Rock lifted his shot pistol straight up and fired into the darkness. Again and again, he pumped away six shots, spaced a foot apart, directly from where the spears had descended. On the fourth shot he heard a groan and then a body appeared out of the darkness, plummeting down just yards from him, where it splattered into a bloody puddle on the cave floor. The ninja—dead as a proverbial doornail, huge rubber suction cups attached to his elbows and knees. He had traversed the very upper regions of the cavern. Rock looked back up for a second. There . . . he must have gone just where the wall meets the ceiling. That narrow corridor of utter blackness where the light of the bulbs didn't penetrate. All for naught, Rockson thought as he stood up. The ninja's stark black uniform was now drenched with blood, turning it a sticky scarlet. There were no magic tricks that were going to pull him out of this one.

"Rockson!" A voice called from out of the narrow tunnels that led out from the cavern into different sections of the subterranean labyrinth that ran beneath Carson and Ice Mountain. The voice yelled out again, this time angrily. "Rockson! Turn and look at your destroyer."

"Oh no, not again," the Doomsday Warrior said with a weary look in his eye. He saw the approaching assassin, moving quickly toward him across the cavern floor.

"You guys don't give up, do you? They must pay you a fortune in overtime."

"Your attempts at humor, Mr. Ted Rockson, are as feeble as your attempts at fighting me will be. I am Tamatsu the Swordsman. I am the best."

The assassin was not a large man, slim with long arms. He wore a dark blue hakama, Japanese-style skirt that flowed around his waist, covering his legs. At his side, its scabbard resting in the red sash that criss-crossed his chest and waist, was a samurai sword.

He pulled it out with a lightning draw and continued quickly forward. The tempered steel blade, hand pounded into shape by master craftsmen in the hills of Japan, glistened with slivers of light from the bulbs. Rock could see that it was as sharp as a razor blade as it turned sideways for a second and almost disappeared from view. And by the way the assassin was swinging the thing around, Rock knew he was good.

There must be a whole goddamned squad of them after me, the Doomsday Warrior thought as he slammed a new clip of shells into his pistol. In the past he had accepted his designation as "Most Wanted Man in America" with humor and pride. But now, as he stepped forward to face as formidable an opponent as he had ever seen, the responsibilities of the office seemed a little tiresome.

Tamatsu suddenly rushed forward screaming *"Kaiii!"* as he whipped the blurring blade at Rockson's skull. Rock fired the twelve-gauge shot-pistol, which sent out its spray of hot death. But somehow the swordsman evaded it, stepping just to the side as he came in swinging, and attacked Rock from a slight angle. The sword flashed down like a bolt of white lightning toward Rockson's chest. The Doomsday Warrior spun on a dime, using a quick jerk of his hips to pull him around in less than a hundredth of a second. The sword flew past him, but caught the very tip of the pistol, sending it flying from his hands.

But the Doomsday Warrior was an expert swordsman himself and had studied not just attack but defensive responses to the sword, in a system called Aikido, in which Chen was a master. Aikido was a soft system, which enabled the user of it to blend in with his opponent's motions, in a perfect harmony of movement. Against the slashing sword of Tamatsu, Rock had no other option open to him. To go face to face against the perfect curved blade of that lethal weapon was to invite annihilation. He would have to go *with* the attack.

Tamatsu grinned darkly as Rockson jumped back several yards and stood facing him, his hands held straight up in front of him, firm yet relaxed.

"Others have tried, but I, Tamatsu, will succeed," the cocky Japanese said as he slowly placed one foot forward at a time, the ankle always turned to the outside for instant footing and lightning strikes. Rockson duplicated his advance, moving the corresponding foot back as Tamatsu advanced, keeping exactly the same space between them. He would make the swordsman attack off balance, draw him forward, and then make his move. He had to cut through the training of the man, force him to make the slightest error.

"Yes Tamatsu, I have heard of you." Rockson said as he kept his body just out of reach of the poised sword held above Tamatsu's face, the point aiming down at the cavern floor at a 45-degree angle. With a twist of his hip, Rockson knew, Tamatsu could whip that sword around and down at hundreds of miles an hour.

The assassin's face brightened. "Ah, so my reputation is worldwide. I am known even in the U.S.S.A."

"Yeah," Rock answered, readying himself for what he hoped would be the response to his next words, "known for having killed your mother and father, raping female goats and urinating on the graves of Tarihawa and Ukidai—your sword style's founders."

The assassin's face grew hard as stone as his entire body seemed to freeze in a state of apoplexy. Then he let out a roar that shook Rockson's eardrums and leaped forward swinging the sword around in a steel wind of death. No man on earth could have avoided that speeding blade, but Rockson had gambled on its coming exactly at that angle and spun around, body pulled low to the ground, and to the side of Tamatsu. The sword flew past Rock's head about a quarter inch above, the breeze from the barely missing blow ruffling his dirty black hair, the white streak in the middle starting to fully grow out once again.

There couldn't be a second chance. Rockson, still crouched down, facing Tamatsu's back, pulled at the man's right ankle and slammed the blade of his hand into the nerve behind the knee. Tamatsu crumbled to the cave floor as if an electric jolt had gone through his leg. He slammed down hard, the sword hand cracking against the floor, sending the sword flying off along the pointed rocks in a hail of spitting sparks. The swordsman pulled his leg with a snap, freeing himself from Rockson's grasp and he jumped to his feet, pulling a second, smaller blade, about a foot long, from inside his blue top. They circled each other, the swordsman's face suddenly less confident, staring at Rockson in disbelief.

"You desworded me," he said with both fear and respect. "No man has done that before."

"No man will again," Rockson said dryly as he waited for the attack. Tamatsu rushed in, ripping the knife around in a figure eight pattern, slicing at every part of Rockson's body. The Doomsday Warrior feinted to the right and as Tamatsu followed, he jumped back to the left, throwing a handful of rock and dust he had gathered in his palm seconds before when lying on the cave floor. The cloud of particles flew into the ninja's eyes, instantly blinding him. Rockson shot in for the kill, slamming his knee up into the man's groin and lifting him off the ground. The assassin screamed out as his testicles burst apart into a bloody sticky soup and dribbled down his legs. But the screaming didn't last for long. As the assassin came down, Rockson ripped his elbow into the man's throat, smashing the larynx, the windpipe and arteries into a fused mass of blood and twisted bone. Tamatsu threw his hand around his throat and then sank slowly to the ground, jerking and twisting wildly, spitting up fountains of bright red blood through his pale lips. Then he was still.

Rock stared down at the motionless form, the hands still clasped around the ripped throat as if he had strangled himself. The eyes were wide open, staring up at the ceiling, and through it into realms only the dead can enter—beyond, beyond, beyond. He had the warrior's face and had been a brave fighter. But why did all these goddamned fighters have to test themselves on him?

The idea depressed Rock immensely as he suddenly visualized endless bouts against those would-be glory boys. But it didn't depress him nearly as much as when he turned to start back to the caved-in tunnel and saw another nine of the assassin warriors—each one decked out in a menacing outfit representing one of the martial arts, each one clutching some death device—and all of them staring at the Doomsday Warrior with eyes of purest malevolence.

Chapter Twenty-one

"Are you guys cheaper to hire by the dozen or what?" Rock asked, letting the shotpistol hang loosely by his side. Not a man answered him as they slowly spread out in a half-circle, and came toward him, bent on nothing less than his obliteration. They wore blacks and reds and blues, silks and khakis. They carried knives and staffs, laser wands, star knives, each holding the weapon of his specialty in front of him, all aimed at the heart of Ted Rockson. He could see with a quick sweeping glance that they were all as well-trained as those he had already faced, or better. They moved with the flowing motionless ease of only those who have spent decades in the pursuit of complete mastery of one of the martial arts.

And he could see something else. That he was a dead man. There was no way in hell he could face up to *all* of them at once. Death, ever at his shoulder, seemed to claw at his flesh, whisper in his ear—that it was time to go. But Rock wasn't quite ready, not without the fiercest fight he had ever put up in his life. He moved very slowly to the side, away from the rock wall behind him, not wanting to get cornered, lose his maneuverability. The semi-circle closed in, raising their blades, their staffs, and cleavers. Rock waited until they were about 20 feet away and then whipped his pistol up in a blurring arc, firing the thing on full-auto, ripping his arm in a streaking circle across the advancing line. Each of the assassins jumped, in a fraction of a second, to the side, moving with the lightning quick reflexes they had mastered. But Rockson, knowing they could beat the shot, had fired *between* them, not *at* them, so as they jumped, several of them leaped into his line of fire, catching the cross-pattern of shot. One of the killers, holding an immense battle axe, collapsed in spasms on the cave floor, the axe dropping down on its wielder, slamming into the huge neck. It buried itself in to the hilt, sending out a geyser of blood from the pulsing artery.

The one in a white silk flowered gown, holding a narrow stick which Rockson recognized as a Tai-Chi wand, and the one carrying a handful of circular saw-blade sized star knives, slapped their hands over small circles of blood that appeared on their uniforms. Hit, but not dead.

But they kept coming. One down, plenty more to go, the Doomsday Warrior thought to himself as he slammed another magazine into the top of the foot-long pistol. It didn't look good, to say the least. But he didn't have much choice. One at a time, one at a time. Even if they all charged, he remembered from his Aikido and Tai Chi training, only one or two could actually reach him at any one moment. He would spin and weave and strike out at whoever was closest. The rest was in God's hands—if He was still around. The Doomsday Warrior pulled out the glistening double-sided bayonet he had taken in Goerringrad and held it in his left hand. He raised both hands and waited for the first man to come. He would be the first one to die.

There was a sudden crashing sound just behind the entire group as if the wall was coming down. They disappeared from Rockson's eyes in a sudden swirling cloud of dust accompanied by the sounds of yelling and firing. Within seconds the dust disappeared again, sucked in by the now functioning ventilation systems of the cave complex. Rock could scarcely believe his eyes. Pouring forth from the caved-in tunnel, which was now cleared of its rocks and boulders, was the rest of the team, their Liberators and pistols at the ready.

"What the hell is going on here?" Detroit yelled out, a huge chromium .45 in his hand.

Chen, Archer and the other six men of the repair team stared wide-eyed at the apparitions of the assassin squad as they slowly reappeared out of the dust cloud.

"I was beginning to feel a little bit like Custer at Little Big Horn," Rock yelled over to his men, now 15 yards away.

"Yeah, we knew you'd be in some sort of trouble, like you always are," Detroit yelled back. "So we blasted the whole damned cave-in apart with some explosives one of the techs remembered were stored nearby."

The assassins looked on in confusion. The cave-in had been created to stop the others from helping. So that there could be no doubt of the outcome. But it didn't matter to them. They were the toughest, the baddest hombres on the face of this earth. A few more split skulls and dismembered bodies would add spice to the historic event—the death of Ted Rockson.

They came suddenly forward at the same instant like a pack of leopards, moving with feline speed. Three of them headed toward Rockson while the others turned to face the Freefighters who had just blasted their way through.

They charged Rockson with grim smiles on their cruel faces—Matsu—the Goju karate master in karate gi with huge spiked brass-knuckles on each of his steel-hard fists; C'hing Chow—the goateed Tai Chi master holding a 24" long Tai Chi wand in his right hand, its ruby laser tip glowing like a white hot coal, ready to send out its death beam; Wing Wu—the White Avenger decked out in a flowing white silk robe that swirled around his legs raised a sword. Each of them was capable of taking on any twenty men—only now their combined energies were directed toward just one—the Doomsday Warrior.

Rock knew he was in for the fight of his life. Against even highly trained fighters, his knowledge of the martial arts and his lightning quick reflexes made it no contest. But against these masters, he'd need every trick in the book to come out on top. He glanced around for a split second and saw that the rest of the assassin squad was breaking up—each heading for one of the Freefighters. His men were tough, but other than Chen, Rock felt a sinking feeling in his gut that they didn't have a chance against these super-fighters. But he didn't have time to worry about the future.

C'hing Chow suddenly charged in, taking tiny steps but somehow moving with the speed of a cheetah. Rock whirled around in a pivot, letting the white-goateed master fly by him. He raised his shot-pistol ready for the next two but saw in a flash that they were standing yards away watching. So they were going to do it one at a time. Their pride, their belief that each was the only one who could do the job, dictated that Rock would be allowed to engage them one at a time. At least for the time being. Their egos were getting in the way of the assassination itself. Well, that was fine with Rock. He had nothing to prove beyond sheer survival. He put his peripheral vision on hold so he wouldn't keep looking out of the corner of his eye, directed all his energies toward the Tai Chi master who had stopped on a dime and was once again coming toward him with those speeding locomotive-like tiny steps. His narrow, golden-toned face was as frozen as the icy face of the moon, and within those black eyes were mirrored the death of hundreds of men.

Rockson again gauged the speed and angle of the robed master and ripped the shot pistol up letting loose two rounds. But somehow the blast missed the assassin even though he was just yards away. C'hing Chow was just *not there*. A flicker of a smile traced through the narrow-lipped mouth as he raised his narrow wand and pointed it at Rockson. A bolt of white light shot out from the throbbing ruby tip as the laser beam sped at the speed of light toward Rockson, hitting him in his pistol hand. He felt a stab of pain on the back of his hand, and the smell of burning flesh—his own, filled his nostrils. The pinpoint laser beam had burned a half-inch hole nearly down to the bone of Rockson's hand. The gun flew out of his spasming fingers and landed nearly eight feet away on the cave floor.

"Shit," Rock spat out as he jumped back, barely avoiding a second flash of blinding light. The beam silently shot past him and into the cavern wall nearly a hundred feet behind him, gouging out a glowing hole in the granite surface. Great—three seconds into the fight and he had already lost his equalizer. But in the game of life and death there can be no time to worry—just fight. He'd have to make do, or die.

"You disappoint me, Mr. Rockson," the Tai Chi master said with the neutral calmness of those who have devoted their lives to killing. "I had expected this fight to be the highlight of my martial career. But now, I hardly think this battle will enter the history books of the fighting arts."

"It's 12 seconds into round one," Rock said, shifting the bayonet to his right hand, which though it throbbed like hell, seemed functional. "I'm the kind of guy that needs to get warmed up."

"Well I'm sure I can oblige you," C'hing Chow said, opening his narrow mouth and releasing an almost inhuman sound that passed for a laugh. "I will not just warm you—but burn you up."

He turned his wrist ever so slightly and another of the deadly laser beams shot out. But this time at last, Rock had felt it coming and again twisted out of the way, just barely avoiding the stream of starfire. He could feel the heat of it brush by his lower back. This is insane, he thought as he jumped to the side and continued spinning, moving out of the way of the beam which tried to follow him like a heat-seeking missile. One after another of the streaking laser shots searched after him, inching in toward his flesh.

The other two killers stood side by side, their arms folded across their chests, watching impassively. They both wished to see Rockson dead, but in their hearts they hoped C'hing Chow would fail and their chance would come. For the man who killed Ted Rockson would reap rewards beyond his dreams—would, at least for a time, be officially designated as the martial artist extraordinaire. And what meant more to them than even the money, the mansion, the women they would receive as reward—for the man who killed the ultimate American would achieve immortality.

Rockson knew he had only seconds before one of the million-degree flashes burnt into him.

Once a knee or throat shot was made, he knew the Tai Chi killer would close in and send out a barrage of beams that would burn him to the bone.

He searched frantically through his mind for a weakness in the assassin. Tai Chi was based on routing—the body sending all its energy down to the ground, centered like a tree in the earth. If he could break the man's contact with the ground, he could deprive him of his power. But like all fighting plans, it was easier thought than done. Rockson was in full evasive maneuvers now, spinning around like a whirling-dervish, constantly changing his location like a mini-tornado that didn't quite know where it was heading. The sizzling white beams shot out again and again barely missing the Doomsday Warrior.

Suddenly Rock stopped in his tracks, sensing the Tai Chi master just behind him. He dropped to the ground, letting his knees fold up like an accordion as a laser burst ripped into the air where his head had been a fraction of a second before. *Now*, it had to *now*. In a half crouch, Rockson vaulted forward with all the power of his iron-muscled legs. He slammed into the assassin's knees buckling them in half. The master fell forward flying over Rock's back and crashed into the granite floor of the cave, instantly trying to regain his balance. But Rockson didn't give him a chance, flipping over with the speed of a tiger and landing on the man's chest, once again knocking him to the ground. C'hing Chow tried to raise the laser wand but Rockson slammed his fist into the man's wrist and the death weapon flew several feet off, rolling over on the stony ground.

The two men looked at each other for the barest moment—each seeing only death in the other's pupils. Then Rock slammed the blade of his right hand down into the assassin's throat. Again and again he struck—five times, crushing the windpipe in a splatter of blood and fragmented adam's apple. C'hing Chow's face took on a look of ultimate surprise—as if it was impossible that this dirty rebel American could have hurt him. Then a fountain of blood erupted from his mouth and he ceased his struggles, as cold and motionless as the stone beneath his back.

Rock rose wearily from the ground, knowing it was just the start. There were two—maybe many more to go, and already he was ready to go home and climb in bed. But he had miles to go and blood to spill before he could rest. He stood straight up and turned. His two waiting adversaries looked on with a certain satisfaction. Now they would get their chance.

Matsu—the Goju Karate master stepped forward, rolling up his thick white-cloth sleeves. "Chow was old and feeble," he said by way of explanation to the Doomsday Warrior. "I am young and powerful. Now—now you will die, Rockson. But I will make it quick for you. Little pain. I wish only to destroy, not to torture."

"Oh how kind," Rock said. "It's nice to fight like humanitarians."

The karate killer came forward, set in a rigid fighting stance, low to the ground, legs wide apart, arms half-crossed with clenched iron-hard fists pointed at the Doomsday Warrior. Though the assassin was about Rockson's height he seemed nearly twice as wide, built like a human rhino, with muscular arms that made Rockson's own steel strength seem like a child's. Rock grabbed his bayonet up from the cavern floor.

The two men circled each other warily, Matsu moving with stamping movements, slamming each foot down with an explosive contact on the ground. His mouth was set in a half-smile, twisting up at the right side as if he found it all quite amusing. Rockson knew his style—Hard Goju—one of the most deadly karate styles ever developed. But also one of the most rigid—without fluidity, based solely on sheer force. Well, let him make his moves, Rock thought as he breathed out, making his own body as relaxed and supple as possible.

Suddenly, as if a fuse had ignited his explosive power, Matsu came forward, a blurring whirlwind of kicks and punches. The speed of the blows amazed the Doomsday Warrior. The man was more than pure muscle, a honed death machine. Rock blocked each blow, keeping as loose as possible, merely slapping the strikes aside. His years of training had taught him that the lightest block will serve to deflect oncoming blows, merely guiding it off in another direction. Let the other put out the strength. Rock had no interest in proving his manhood.

But the ceaseless stream of lightning-fast kicks and roundhouse kicks was almost impossible to keep up with as the Doomsday Warrior backed off, trying to protect himself. Matsu feinted with a forward kick and then stopped, spinning his whole body around with a backward spinning kick. The blow caught Rock in the solar plexus, lifting him right off the ground and sending him flying backward a good six feet. He landed on his back, rolled over and in a flash was up again. Matsu turned to the third assassin standing nearby and grinned. "I think it will soon be all over." The white silk-robed Kung Fu master stood expressionless. He had seen many fights. This one was not over. And Matsu was showing the Achilles heel of many a great fighter—overconfidence.

Rockson sensed it too, the ego of the man, so sure that he was undefeatable. The Doomsday Warrior knew that the way to fight a man was not to battle his strength but to bring out his weaknesses. A plan formed in Rock's mind, a long shot, but all that he had. He again began circling Matsu, holding the glimmering bayonet blade straight out in his hand. The Goju fighter's foot flashed up like a rattler and slammed the blade into the air, spinning it end-over-end to the floor yards away. Instantly Matsu closed in again, releasing a windmill of punches and kicks. Rock blocked each one, spinning his hands in tight circles, guiding each strike off to the side. But the man's energy was amazing as he just kept coming forward, a nonstop, one-man armada.

Rock made a move to the left and as Matsu followed, jumped to the opposite side, letting loose his own stiff side kick at the assassin's stomach. But the Goju assassin's defensive reflexes were as finely honed as his attack. He met the kick with a stiff elbow block, slamming Rockson's leg around, nearly throwing him to the ground.

So much for that, Rock thought to himself, impressed more than anything with the man's speed. He had thought Chen one man as fast, or possibly faster than himself. But this overmuscled killer was as quick as anyone he had ever encountered in his entire life. His defense seemed impenetrable. Time for Plan B. Rock took a step backward regaining his balance as Matsu once again came forward, an unending storm of feet and fists. This time, the Doomsday Warrior let the blows come into contact with him, catching them with his hands at the very last second. The timing had to be perfect or he would take the full brunt. He backed off, pulling his head sharply to the side as if being struck by the full force. Matsu advanced, thinking he was destroying Rockson as it seemed that virtually all his strikes were making contact. Rockson's head snapped around again and again, his body half bent over as Matsu's foot slammed into his stomach. The Goju assassin pushed Rock all the way back to the far cave wall, with a punishing barrage of blows. Why, he was virtually destroying the man. Was this the great Ted Rockson—the toughest Freefighter in America? Matsu barked out a contemptuous laugh and came in for the deathblow. With Rock's back right up against the stone wall, Matsu planted his right foot solidly on the ground and let loose with a cannon-like explosion from his left leg. The kick seemed to glue Rock to the wall, his eyes rolling in his head. He threw his arms over his face as if seeking protection and sank slowly to the ground in apparent defeat.

Matsu stood looking down at the "Great Warrior" with a wide smirk. "Bye-bye Ted Rockson, I'll see you in hell."

He raised his foot to slam down on the Doomsday Warrior's head and suddenly felt a surge of electric pain shoot through his right knee as Rockson's foot shot up like a rocket and smashed the knee-cap into fragments. Matsu fell to the floor, instantly pulling himself backward, out of range of his opponent. They both rose and faced each other, Matsu hobbling on the leg. His eyes suddenly seemed stripped of their superiority and filled with a dark fear that Matsu had never before known. No man had ever damaged him before. He edged backward from Rockson whipping out a cloth strip from beneath his gi and wrapping it around the knee so he could walk.

As Rockson slowly advanced on his would-be

killer, Matsu reached behind him and pulled out two steel brass knuckles from a sheath. He slipped them on his hands, formidable looking weapons with four long spikes, sharp as icepicks.

"A lucky strike," Matsu said with a touch more respect in his voice, not wanting to admit the possibility that Rockson had faked being hurt to draw him in. The Doomsday Warrior advanced slowly, watching the fists of the Goju killer with hawk-like eyes. He knew Matsu's kicking attack was down to nil but his fists would be as fast as ever—and with those spike knuckles, Rock couldn't afford to take even one blow. They circled each other like wolves about to lunge for the kill. Suddenly Matsu made his move, jumping forward on his good leg and releasing a volley of rapier-like punches toward Rockson. The Doomsday Warrior didn't even try to block the blows—with the spike knuckles he couldn't take a chance of snagging his wrist or hand on them, but instead evaded each one, twisting and turning as he again edged backward, this time away from the wall, drawing Matsu on. The assassin's mobility was somewhat diminished but the strength of the damaged leg itself, now that it was bound, seemed unaffected.

As if to reassert his strength, Matsu went into a series of Katas—lightning fast moves from the Goju system, flexing into different attack modes to show Rockson the speed and power of his system. It was designed to frighten, but with the Doomsday Warrior, it did the opposite—it showed him an opening. For Rockson knew the Katas too, having worked on them with Chen. And he knew that the double fist strike came right after the windmill dragon parry. He waited, every muscle in his body coiled, ready to strike. Matsu spun both arms around at full length and then shot out with both fists straight ahead simultaneously. Rockson was ready. He grabbed Matsu's wrists as they came out like arrows toward him, locking onto them with all the strength of his veined hands. At the same instant he grabbed hold he jumped up with both legs, slamming them into Matsu's chest and fell backward. As he fell to the ground on his back he kicked the assassin up and over him so the killer fell hard on his back on the icy cavern floor behind Rockson. But Rock didn't give him a chance to rise—somersaulting backward and coming down with all the momentum of his body with the heel of his booted foot on Matsu's head. The face split open from chin to forehead in a gush of blood as the cracked frontal part of the skull exploded out in a spray of teeth and bone. Rock kicked again, and then again, knowing that the assassin would keep coming until his last breath. One of the killer's eyes popped out as the heel slammed into it, dropping down the side of the bloody face, dangling on thin blue veins. The third kick opened up the brain itself and pink liquidy tissue spilled out over Rockson's leg.

Matsu was dead. The Doomsday Warrior rose once again, not wanting to turn, not wanting to face his next, and somehow he sensed, his most formidable, adversary.

Chapter Twenty-two

Across the wide cavern the rest of the Freefighters were in for the fight of their lives, as they waded into battle with the martial arts assassins. Two of the technicians bravely charged at the Smasher—an immense man nearly 7-feet tall, who carried a mallet in one hand, nearly four-feet long and in the other, a huge double-sided cleaver that looked as if it had butchered many a man into strips of bloody meat. Their attempts were noble, but shortlived, as they fell to the cave floor in bloody heaps.

The Smasher turned to face his next opponent, letting forth a deep belly laugh as he saw the diminutive Chen standing with his hands loosely held out in front of him. This would be short work, the killer thought, then he would join the others across the floor who were having their problems with The Rockson.

"Puny fool," the Smasher roared out. "Prepare to die!" He lunged forward, slamming the 40 pound head of the mallet at Chen's head. But somehow the

Oriental Freefighter wasn't there when it arrived. The Smasher charged again, whipping both of his devastating weapons around like battle axes searching for Chen's skull. But each time they descended they merely whistled through empty air as Chen danced around the killer, who outweighed him two-to-one. He could see the man was strong as an ox, but slow. Let him do his thing for a minute, Chen thought to himself, then I'll do mine. He retreated a step at a time as the Smasher furiously sought him out, his mallet veering off for a moment to smash in the skull of another of the untrained technicians who tried to help. The tech fell to the cold floor, his brains dripping over his face and mouth as the assassin once again turned his attentions to the Chinese.

Chen could see the giant was growing frustrated as his blows were continuously missing. He saw his opening—and took it. The assassin charged forward slamming with both of his weapons at the same moment pulling himself slightly off balance. Chen came in from the side landing three roundhouses kicks in a row to the heart side of the man's chest. The blows knocked the wind from the Smasher, pushing him backward a few steps. He grunted and instantly came at the Oriental again in an animal rage. The wilder the better, Chen thought as he timed his next strike. The instant the man's right foot came pounding down on the rock floor, Chen whipped his foot around in a wide circle just inches above the ground, knocking the Smasher flat on his back. He was on him in a flash, like a tiger on its prey. The assassin's thick bull-like neck was too thickly muscled to even try to damage it. Instead Chen went for the softer tissue—the eyes. He made spear hands with the fingers of each hand, tightening them so they were stiff as knives and drove them with all his strength down into the eye sockets. The fingers ripped through the moist tissue and in a good five inches so that Chen could feel the sticky brain tissue sliding apart beneath his blow.

He pulled his hands out, sucking out a swamp of the pink tissue with a loud slurping sound. He rose without looking down. He had scarcely gotten to his feet when he heard a whistling sound—a sound he knew well—a star knife bearing down on him like a meteorite from hell. He threw himself up and into the air in a full body twist, coming down a yard away as a five-pointed metal blade screamed by him and off into the flickering darkness of the cave. Chen turned to see a man about his size, also Oriental, in skin-tight purple plastic body suit, his hands loaded with the deadly throwing blades. The assassin flicked his right hand and sent out two more of the buzzsaws at Chen who barely evaded them by dropping flat on his face as they spun by overhead. He had never seen a man so adept, so quick with the star knives except for his own Master—Wu Su—and himself. As he rolled over and over on the cold stone ground Chen whipped out four of his own death stars from beneath his jacket, gripping two of them tightly in each hand. He came up to one knee and flicked out one of them toward another of the assassin's steel blades that was coming in at him. They met in mid-air, slamming into one another, sending sparks flying and then fell to the ground. Hu Chang, The Starknife looked at his opponent with a sudden wariness. The man should have been dead already. Only Rockson was supposed to be a worthy opponent—and yet . . .

Hu Chang retreated behind a rock pillar and unleashed another two of the pointed knives. They flew through the air like rockets inches apart. But Chen spun and dodged, heading straight toward the assassin's cover. Suddenly the Starknife killer was in full retreat, running as fast as his legs could carry him until he reached the cavern wall—and there was nowhere left to run. He turned, pulling out another handful of the blades and prepared to unleash them. He never got the chance as one of Chen's deathstalkers spun through the air and buried itself in the assassin's chest. Only this one was an exploding blade, created by Dr. Shecters' weapons team, a mixture of steel and plastique. It exploded upon contact with the killer's chest and sent out a hail of bloody bone in all directions. Hu Chang looked down at his open chest and stared with horror at the still beating heart that lay exposed within, half falling out of the huge hole where the rib cage had been a second before. Then he toppled over falling onto the bloody flesh that had preceded him.

Seventy-five feet away Detroit was edging back from the Red Avenger—cloaked in a shimmering red silk brocaded gown. The man whipped out a gold bladed sword and pushed a button at the bottom of the hilt. The single blade suddenly sprang into four blades, each nearly four feet long, all joined at the handle. Detroit gulped once and fired his .45 twice.

But the assassin spun the four blades of his weapon around in a blur of motion and deflected the streaking slugs. Then he came in for the kill, whirling the blades like an airplane propeller, heading right for Detroit's neck who fortuitously bumped into a small stalagmite and fell backward. The swords whizzed by and the attacker screamed out a roar of victory. But the roar was too soon. The Red Avenger saw in an instant that he had missed and whipped the golden swords down at Detroit, who floundered around the ground trying to avoid the slashing blades. One of them ripped down the side of his leg slicing his thick work pants in two and leaving an inch deep wound nearly a foot long which began leaking a stream of blood. Somehow the black Freefighter managed to stagger to his feet just out of range of his attacker, his dark skin coated with an icy sweat.

He knew he couldn't take many more attacks—the man was just too fast even for Detroit's quick reflexes. He shot out another three slugs but again the golden blades whirled faster than the eye could see and the bullets ricocheted off gold/tungsten/manganese surface with loud pings. A large smile crossed the Red Avenger's face as he came in for the death blow. He liked killing and had never liquidated a black before. It would make a nice addition to his quarters back in Moscow, where he burned a different colored candle on his death altar, commemorating each of his kills. He would light a black candle when he returned, for his negro.

The assassin sped forward, seeing that Detroit had unknowingly backed himself against one of the cave's huge stalagmites that ran from the ground up to the cavern's ceiling, slashing the four blades down with all his strength—and hit paydirt. One of the razor-sharp edges ripped into Detroit's arm just above the elbow, severing the appendage cleanly. It fell to the ground with a sickening thump as the black Freefighter fought to keep from sliding into shock. He turned his head down and saw the stump that was now his left arm and nearly fainted. There's something about seeing part of your body sliced off that has a somewhat drastic effect on one's outlook. But he was still alive—and like all Freefighters—he would fight to the last. The .45 was empty although it hadn't seemed to have any effect on the killer anyway. Using every bit of mental and physical strength that he possessed, Detroit reached around with his good arm and grabbed one of two grenades he had put in his jacket before leaving Century City—his weapon of expertise—with which he was never without. This was his last shot and he knew it.

The Red Avenger lifted the swords high over his head in a dramatic pose, savoring the moment of murder. It was this instant that he lived for—when he took another man's life—when he could feel the life force leave the corpse he had just created—sense the soul departing its lifeless shell and heading down into whatever hell awaited below. But his moment of high theatrics was his only mistake. Detroit saw the hovering swords and made his move. He leaped forward, pulling the pin of the grenade and stuffed it deep into the Avenger's 20,000 ruble silk gown. At the same moment he kicked as hard as he could against the assassin's leg, sending the man tumbling to the ground, his sword flying from his grasp. As the killer hit the dirt, Detroit jumped on his back swinging his good arm around the man's throat and pulling with all his strength. The Avenger reached up and tried to pry himself free and had just ripped Detroit's weakening arm away when the grenade went off. To Detroit, on top, it felt like he was riding a bucking bronco for a split second as the assassin's entire body shot off the floor, nearly two feet into the air. Then it dropped back down again, a shattered bloody hulk. Detroit rolled off the dead thing beneath him and stared at it. There was hardly anything left on the front side that was recognizable as a man—just oozing slime and pieces of organs pasted over the body like a bad paint job. The black Freefighter ripped off a strip of the red silk outfit and tied a tourniquet around his bleeding stump. Then he crawled over to a stalagmite and collapsed against it unable to move another inch. His eyes barely open, he watched the continuing conflagration around him.

As the assassin team broke up to engage their Freefighter opponents, Archer found himself face to face with a much smaller man, wearing short, cut-off gray pants and leather vest. The half mute grinned as he saw who he would fight—for the fellow was surely no match for the strongest man in Century City—whatever kung fu he knew. But as Archer came in swinging his hamhock-sized fists, looking for a quick end to it, he grew quickly concerned. Wherever he struck the smaller man spun away. Kenoi—Master of the Monkey Form went into a peculiar stance, his legs bent at the knees as if he could hardly stand up, his arms held out dangling ahead, the fists unclenched like loose fruits about to fall. The killer's face was completely expressionless, just his eyes showing a coldness as frigid as the depths of space itself. As Archer came in for a third attack trying to grab the nearly foot shorter assassin, Kenoi whipped one of his almost rope-like arms around and the loose fist snapped up and into Archer's face, cracking two of his teeth. The giant staggered backward in shocked surprise. No man had ever hit him that hard before—not even The Rockson—and this was just a string bean of a man compared to his own 7 foot plus, 400 pound stature. With a roar of primitive rage he came forward again, wanting to destroy the man who had dared attack him, with the mindless bravery of a beast.

But against the super honed skills of Kenoi, the giant's blows were completely ineffectual. The Monkey Form, based on observations of the movements of monkeys centuries before by the buddhist founders of the form, used relaxation and long circular punches to get through its opponent's defenses. For every punch Archer threw—and missed—the assassin seemed to get in two or three. The huge Freefighter could feel the blows beginning to take their toll. It was like being struck by lightning, each punch rocking the near-mute through to his very backbone. He slowed down for a second or two trying to calm himself. He had always relied on sheer brute strength to get the job done, but for the first time in his life he could sense that that would not be enough.

He tried to think like Rockson. The Doomsday Warrior had tried to teach him some of the martial arts but Archer had just scoffed. Now he desperately searched through his mind for something—anything—that would get him through the toughest battle he had ever faced. Softness Rockson had always told him that if he could train his body to relax—to strike with a loose punch using all his body weight, he could knock down trees. Archer sank down on his legs, breathed out and held up his arms in imitation of Kenoi, long and loose in the Monkey style. The assassin laughed out loud for the first time in all his years of killing men. The clumsy imitation the giant was trying to make of the deceptively simple-looking Monkey form was quite absurd—every angle wrong, every alignment of the joints out of place. Well, it was his choice how he chose to die.

The smile abruptly vanished from Kenoi's face as he came in with a barrage of his incredibly powerful wide circular punches. But somehow, as clumsy as his blocks were, the sheer relaxing of Archer's body nearly doubled his speed. For the first time he understood what Rockson had been trying to teach him. By unclenching the muscles of his arm and fist he could add tremendous speed and focus to his punches. He shot out his right fist, letting it just hang out in front of him like a slow flying bird—and lo and behold—it made contact with Kenoi's chest, knocking the assassin back a good yard. A beaming smile crossed Archer's face. There, now he was getting somewhere. But only for a second as Kenoi went into overdrive and unleashed a flurry of roundhouse punches that got through Archer's blocks. Three of them slammed into the side of his head, almost dropping him. But he knew that if he went down, he wasn't going to get up again. He couldn't take many more—he'd have to take a chance, take a few of the strikes to get in one of his own.

The bear of a Freefighter retreated for the first time he had ever fought, remembering how Rockson and Chen had moved like waves of water against each other—the hard into the soft, the yin and the yang. Kenoi breathed out an explosive exhale and came in for the coup de grace, sensing Archer's dizziness. Just a step further, the giant thought, just a step. As the assassin flew forward with another maelstrom of blinding punches, Archer also jumped forward meeting him in mid air. He took two of the blows on the side of his neck but not enough to stop him. He lowered his head and slammed the top of it into the Monkey stylist's face. The nose crunched in like a piece of bloody cardboard as half the man's teeth flew from his face, sprinkling onto the ground. Kenoi's arms flew out wide as he stumbled backward half out on his feet. But Archer wasn't going to allow him a second chance. He dove on top of the man, knocking him to the ground and with his immense weight pinning the assassin down slammed the top of his head again and again into the bloody face, goring at it like a maddened bull. He whipped his skull down over and over, not even knowing quite what he was doing. His hair and face covered with the assassin's blood, Archer at last stopped and sat up on top of the body ready to strike again if the man made the slightest move. But there was no counter-attack. There was nothing. The face had been shattered down to red pulp, the tongue half bitten off by the slapping jaws of Kenoi, the nose gone, the eyes just bloody balls floating in a dark liquid.

Not knowing how the rest of his team was faring, Rockson rose from the lifeless body of his karate opponent and turned to face the smallest of his assassin attackers, an aged man almost frail-looking in a white silk robe. Rock's body ached like the devil already—and God only knew how many more there were to go. A quick glance around the cavern showed him only men fighting fiercely with one another, bodies covered with blood. But in the dim flickering illumination from the string of bulbs along one wall it was impossible to see who was doing what to whom.

"Ted Rockson—I am the White Fan," the elderly assassin said, addressing the Doomsday Warrior in polite almost conversational tones as he fanned himself with a white oriental fan with pictures of dragons and tigers in wild colors drawn on its surface. "I have no animosity toward you—you understand," the killer went on. "I can see that you are a brave and accomplished fighter. But I have my duty to perform. So please prepare your thoughts for death. The others were tough—but I assure you that I am at an entirely different level."

"Can't we talk about all this?" Rock asked, his body begging him not to push it any further. "You seem like a civilized man, perhaps—"

"Save your breath—and your strength, Mr. Rockson. I cannot back down. Nor can you. Shall we proceed?" He walked toward the Doomsday Warrior with a simple slow gait, appearing to the untrained eye to be nothing more than an old and skinny man. But Rockson knew differently. The assassin moved with total relaxation, every muscle, every nerve in his body, moving together in perfect harmony. But it was the eyes that were the giveaway—pools of unfathomable green, absolute stillness, like the surface of the moon. Eyes that were a mirror—eyes of the True Master.

"Shit," Rockson half muttered through a bloody lip. He just wasn't in the mood for this. But death didn't sent out calling cards R.S.V.P.—it had a habit of showing up on one's doorstep unannounced, quickly bringing an end to the part of life. But he was in even less of a mood to die, so the Doomsday Warrior wearily lifted the bayonet blade and went into fighting stance, his legs half crouched for quick movement.

"Yes, you see I am the last of the real Masters," the White Fan said, casually waving the fan in front of his face as if he were out on the veranda trying to create a cooling breeze. "The others—well—you shall see soon enough for yourself." Seeing an opportunity as the assassin spoke, Rock lunged forward fast as a cobra, thrusting the long blade at the man's stomach. But the fan simply dropped down in the most casual of motions and knocked his hand away.

"It is really quite pitiful, Mr. Rockson, for you see I can sense every motion you are going to make," the aged, white-faced killer said, "and counter it." Rock jumped to the side trying to flank the man. But even as he moved the White Fan spoke again.

"Now you are moving at a 45 degree angle to cut off my circular movement. Now you will thrust again." And as Rockson shot out the blade in a sure death blow, the assassin once again merely batted it away as if hitting a fly. "You are fast—but not fast enough. I train with the wind, Rockson, with the animals of the field." He was suddenly right up against the Doomsday Warrior, almost hugging his body, just inches away. The fan swung up suddenly folding closed and slammed Rockson in the face. It felt like a spear had ripped into him as a burning pain filled his skull.

"Like this and—" the White Fan said, dropping his fan to waist level and stabbing forward twice into Rockson's stomach, "like this. There, you see how easy it all is." Rock almost doubled over from the blow to his solar plexus, sucking in deep breaths. "Ah, sometimes I wish there was someone who could give me a real fight. It gets—boring." The White Fan came at Rockson, spinning the now opened fan in front of him like a toreador's cape, creating a dizzying blur of white. And again the Doomsday Warrior felt the seemingly harmless implement slam into him. Shots hit his face and throat and stomach in an unending barrage of blows sending Rock reeling backward as if he had been struck by a cannon shell. He fell down, landing on his back, not even able to soften the blow with his arms. He could feel his consciousness going out like a fading lightbulb. He had never felt so awkward, so humiliated. He couldn't even touch the man. All his years of training, of fighting meant nil against one of the last living Masters. Rock tried to rise from a sitting position and found his body barely responding to his commands. Even flesh and muscle as toughened as

Rockson's had its limits. He wasn't a superman—just a man—and a very mortal one at that.

The White Fan stood looking down at him from about 8 feet away in no apparent hurry to end it all. He smiled an almost pitying expression at the Doomsday Warrior.

"Have no shame, Mr. Rockson—none have ever beaten me. None ever will. At least die knowing that you have been destroyed by the best—the very best." He started forward in that slow almost childlike gait toward Rockson, spreading the fan out and raising it for the slicing stroke that would cut through Rockson's throat.

The Doomsday Warrior suddenly realized that his left hand was resting on something hard and glanced over—one of the spiked brass knuckles from the Goju Master. He slid his hand around the smooth grip and tightened his fingers around it. Though God knew what good it would do against a man whose defenses were totally impenetrable. As he backed off, Rockson felt a small button at the thumb of the knucks. The weapon obviously had another level of operation set into motion by pushing the almost invisible button. But whether it would blow him or the other guy away, Rockson had no way of testing. He had nothing to lose—that was for damned sure.

He whipped the hand up and around as the White Fan descended with his death blow, and pushed the button. Rock's hand shook as if resting on a bazooka as all four of the three-inch long steel spikes shot out of the knuckles like bullets. They streaked through the air reaching the White Fan, who was only a foot away, in a thousandth of a second. All four steel shafts buried themselves deep in the assassin's chest, inches apart, sinking in so only the last half inch of their bottoms poked out. The White Fan's hand stopped in mid-air as if hitting a slab of steel and he looked quite surprised as four streams of blood began flowing messily down the front of his spotless white robe. Then he looked at Rockson again.

The White Fan's legs suddenly turned to rubber and he staggered back, a tiny step at a time. The thinnest of smiles arched across his narrow mouth as if even in death he felt a perverse joy at having finally fought a worthy adversary. Then he crumpled to the ground, nothing more than another corpse which littered the cavern floor.

Rock rose to his feet, his face throbbing and beginning to swell up from the thunderous blows he had taken from the Master. His right knee seemed to have been hurt somewhere along the line and he limped slightly as he started toward the center of the cavern where the fighting was still going on.

There were just two assassins left—one a young bull of a fighter holding a pair of steel-tipped nun-chaks in each hand, spinning them in a blurring flash around in front of him. The other, an older Chinese, dressed entirely in black, who stood crouched in a strange scissor leg type motion, his body turned sharply at the waist, hands out front—a style that Rockson recognized as Pa Kua. The rest of the Freefighters were surrounding them as the two drew close together suddenly realizing that their "sure victory" over Ted Rockson had turned into a disaster of ultimate proportions.

The young bull, Duk Sung, a Korean, started at Rockson who was approaching, swinging the deadly nunchaks toward the Freefighter's throat. But a whistling star knife stopped him in his tracks as it arched into his throat, burying the 5-pointed blade a good four inches into the thick flesh. The Korean gagged as both of his sticks dropped from his suddenly paralyzed hands. Then he spat out a violent spray of blood that filled the air in front of him and fell straight over onto his face, nose just inches from Rockson's foot.

"No sense in any more of us getting hurt," Chen said, walking over, holding one of the star killers in his other hand. "You all right Rock?" the Oriental fighter asked, noticing blood splattered over Rock's face and chest and the limp in his leg.

"I'm still here," the Doomsday Warrior said tiredly. "That's more than the guys I fought can say." The two of them turned simultaneously toward the final remaining assassin who continued to circle in front of them, kicking one leg out at the knee, stepping forward, then placing the other in what looked like an awkward motion. But the off balance walk, Rockson knew, was part of perhaps the most efficient martial art ever devised. This fighter could well be the most dangerous of them all.

"There's no need to fight me," the man suddenly said in almost perfect English as he stopped his defensive posturings and rose to a normal standing position. "I am Yi—Master of the Scissor Kick and the Iron Fist Systems. We have lost—you have won. It is clear. To the victor goes life—to the vanquished, death. This is as it has always been and always shall be. I ask only that you permit me to die by my own hand—as a warrior so that I may join my ancestors and my Master."

Rock and Chen looked at each other as Archer and the surviving technician stood behind them.

"What the hell," Chen said, "if he wants to—let him."

"I don't feel like doing any more killing today," Rockson said, putting a hand onto Chen's shoulder for support as his knee filled with a shooting electric stab of pain. The Pa Kua Master immediately knelt and bowed to all four points of the compass. Then he took out a small but razor sharp blade and opening the top of his black jacket, pressed the knife right up to his flesh just two inches below his bellybutton. He pulled in as hard as he could and began slicing around in all directions. Suddenly his neck stiffened and his head arched up as his intestines slopped out onto the cave floor. His eyes nearly bursting in their sockets he fell forward into the bloody pool of his own guts.

"Well, I guess that's just about—" Rock started to say but stopped in mid-sentence as he looked around. "Where's Detroit?" His face grew pale at the thought that the black Freefighter might have bought it. They looked around frantically, searching through the bodies of the dead assassins.

"I'm over here," a weak voice spoke out from the opposite end of the cavern. The Freefighters ran over and found him half-lying, half-sitting against a tree-sized stalagmite nearly three feet wide at the base.

"I got a little cut here," the black warrior said with

a grimace. In the flickering light of the bulbs yards away they suddenly saw that Detroit's arm was gone, cut from the elbow down. "I wish they'd got the other one, cause this here's my pitching arm." He motioned with his eyes to the missing limb which lay covered in dust and blood near his feet.

"Pick him up," Rock said to Archer who bent down and lifted the bulldog of a black Freefighter gently in his huge arms. The Doomsday Warrior reached down and picked up the hacked off limb, immediately cleaning it with water from a crevice stream a few feet away and then tied the open end closed with cord. He wrapped the arm in one of the silk jackets from a dead assassin. The team tore back to Century City, shooting down the tunnels they'd come through earlier, following Chen's trail of nylon line, every man praying silently that Detroit would make it.

Behind them, the first of the rats, the large aggressive males, ventured forth from dank holes to sniff at the unmoving bodies that lay strewn around the cavern. They circled the corpses at first, for the lift scents were very strong. They had to be careful. But after several minutes, a foot-and-a-half long creature with curved ivory fangs inches long, rushed suddenly forward and sank its jaws into the face of the White Fan. It ripped out a bloody strip of the cheek and swallowed it down greedily. The others quickly joined it.

Chapter Twenty-three

After Detroit had been delivered to the operating room in the Century City hospital, its systems all functioning now with the power restored, Rock headed step by dragging step down to his room. His mind was full with a storm of thoughts and emotions—primarily that Detroit would regain use of his arm. The head surgeon, Johnston, had told him that the black Freefighter would definitely survive—but whether or not he would be able to reattach the limb was another question. They had only been using the sophisticated micro-surgery techniques for a few years and had never put back an entire arm before. But Rock knew he was the best—if it could be done the surgical team would do it. And beneath his concern about Detroit, the realization that Century City's defenses had been breached by the assassins. Had they been alone so that the secret of the free city's location died with them or—he shuddered to even think of it—did the Reds now know where they were. He couldn't face the prospect of another battle like the one he had just been through or 10,000 Red Army troops trying to battle their way inside.

But by the time he reached his room, his brain was too tired to think of anything as he fell in a heap on his bed. Within seconds he was in a deep sleep—a sleep that should have been dreamless for the exhausted seldom dream.

But his sleep wasn't dreamless. There was a nightmare, a nightmare as chilling as anything Rockson had ever experienced. Rock's door was locked from the inside—pickproof—with an alarm system. Yet in the dream, someone opened the door silently and entered. A dark figure—a blackness beneath a glowing skull that seemed to drift bodiless above the floor. The skull floated toward the fuse box, opened it and unscrewed the fuse from its socket. The skull slowly turned and approached the bed.

Rock mumbled in his sleep, "no, no," tossing and turning as his exhausted mind tried to rid the dream of this horror. There was the sound of slow deep breathing, a sort of hiss above the Doomsday Warrior's bed, as the skull floated toward him. Rock dreamed that he got up and was standing next to the bed, but his feet were stuck to the floor, his body paralyzed. He tried to move but the most titanic efforts only turned him around, his feet glued to the concrete floor as surely as if they had been cast in cement. He struggled for breath, trying to wake himself—for something inside told him it was all real.

But a voice spoke to him, a hypnotic voice, saying "*Sleep, relax, you are sleeping. There is no danger.*" The voice hissed a cold stream of air between its skull teeth.

Something was wrong. The dream was too controlled, too calculated. With an enormous effort of will, Rockson opened his eyes and saw the skull hanging over the bed, a death moon floating in black space. Or was he still dreaming? Dreaming that he had awakened. He tried to clear his foggy consciousness. Everything was spinning, reality, unreality, a fog of incomprehension. Rockson felt a deadly lethargy coming over him, descending like a blanketing cloud over his senses. And all the while, the mesmerizing, droning voice that seemed to reach into the very core of his nervous system, saying, "*Relax, it's just a dream. This is not real. Just a dream.*"

He felt himself going under the power of the dark energy, and rubbed his eyes, trying to keep them focused on the wavery apparition. From deep inside himself a voice cried out. "*It is real; Danger! It has come to kill you! Wake up! Must wake up*!"

"It's real," he shouted to himself, forcing his body to awaken from the dream that was also a reality. He jumped out of bed naked, throwing the billowing sheet toward the assassin. That broke the spell. The skull apparition ripped the floating sheet from the air, shredding it into tatters and with a single swipe of its clawed hand leapt forward toward where Rock had been lying, slashing the bed in half with a long glowing sword blade, nearly six feet long with a burning red stream of fire arching out from its tip. The bedding burst into flame, the mattress stuffing erupting in a hundred little tongues of fire.

Rockson dove forward and hit the floor the other side of his assailant, somersaulting across the room toward the closet where his .12 gauge shotpistol hung, a new one from the small arms depot. He grabbed it from a wire hook, turned and fired point blank at the skull faced killer. Nothing! The skull, which seemed to float in the darkness of the room lit only by the now smoldering mattress had a shadowy body beneath it, sleek as a leopard's. The skull opened its bone jaws and laughed a deep echoing sound as if from the grave itself.

"*Fool*," the skull spoke, "*You cannot kill a ghost. You cannot destroy me—rather it is I who will destroy you.*"

"Like hell you will," Rock said, taking a star knife from the back of the shotpistol's holster and whirling it toward the deathly figure. He heard a howl and thought he saw a trickle of blood. The thing, whatever it was, apparently had some form of forcefield deflector for bullets—but not for the much slower alloy star knives. At least he knew the thing *could* be hurt.

The skull suddenly vanished into the very shadows. Then there was a scuffling, like a rat along the floor. Rockson was pulled from his feet before he had a chance to react. Only a snap roll to the side, throwing his entire body weight over, broke the skeletal grip around his left ankle. The glowing fire sword again sliced through the air at him, missing his chest by inches.

The eyes of the thing began throbbing with a green/red fire. Those eyes, the eyes—he was drawn to them like a moth to flame, unable to withstand the hypnotic pull. The wide empty orbs with pulsating red pupils in the center, pupils that drew Rock in like a whirlpool, sucking at his mind. He tried to break free of the eyes—but couldn't. The voice began speaking again in a slow, irresistible monotone.

"You are me and I am you . . . If you kill me—you will die. If I feel pain you will feel it." Rock felt his will slipping away. He took the other star knife he had grabbed in his right hand, and straining as if he were lifting a truck, managed to raise it and jam it into his own right forearm. The sudden jolt of pain drove the dreamlike state from his head. *There—your mind is clear*, he thought in the first moment of clarity he had had since the nightmare began. *Act now, now!*

Rock threw the final circular blade. The spinning five-pointed knife hit the assassin just below the skull—and whizzed on into the darkness imbedding itself in the wall. *How the hell did he do that? Its neck should have been there.* The mad laughter that came back at him sent chills down his spine.

"Mortal, you think I am human? That you can kill me? Suddenly three skulls appeared in the air, one right next to the other. "*Which one of me is the reality? Which the illusion*? the skull laughed. *"Give up, Rockson. There is no hope for you. None. Die peacefully. Go to the next world where there is eternal peace.*

But Rockson just didn't feel like dying peacefully. If he had to go—it would be violently. He had to take a chance. One of the skulls coming in on him, one of the raised glowing sceptres was real. But which one? Which? His sixth sense told him to go for the center one. He lunged forward—and made contact with something solid. The ghost—or whatever the hell it was—wheezed out air, the breath knocked out of it. Rock wrapped his arms around the thing and wouldn't let go—even when the huge electro-blade roared down through the air at him. He grabbed the wrist that held the sword and twisted it, making the boney flesh drop it. The blade fell to the floor, digging into the solid concrete, burning a hole, from which it stuck upright, swinging slightly back and forth. His clothes, lying on the floor next to the glowing weapon, suddenly caught fire and in the flash from the flames he could see the thing trying to kill him. It was a man—not a ghost, not a supernatural being. A magician of some sort wearing a skin tight black body suit, with the outline of a skeleton on it—but a man, a human, who could be killed.

The assassin broke away toward the door and Rockson rushed after him, grabbing up the sword from the floor. He took one huge step and swung the singing fire-blade down with all his might. The blade entered the killer's skull and continued down through his body, exiting from the groin and continuing its downward stroke until it was buried sideways in the floor. The assassin's body, cleanly split in two spouted a wall of blood and fell to both sides, all the inner organs, the heart and lungs flopping out onto the floor where they writhed and pulsated like fish out of water. Then all was once again silent. Rock felt himself growing dizzy and glanced over to see that his burning clothes had set the bedsheets and bureau on fire. He felt himself passing out and somehow managed to crawl on his hands and knees toward the door, which he somehow pulled open. The smoke alarms in the hall went off just as he passed out.

When he awoke Rona was standing next to him holding his hand. He was lying in a hospital bed, the stiffly starched sheets smooth and cool against his aching flesh.

"How do you feel?" she asked softly. He pressed her hand.

"Fine," he said weakly, but he sounded hoarse, his throat burned.

Dr. Johnston walked over, hearing him speak. "I'm glad to see you're back among the sordid world of the living," he smiled. "You really do have nine lives. I saw the man you killed. And the fire squad had a hell of a time putting out that fire. It consumed the entire room before they extinguished it. You'll have to tell me what the hell happened in there."

"Some other time," Rona said firmly.

"Yeah," Rock joined in. "Some other time. Say doc, could we—Rona and I have a little privacy."

Doctor Johnston whistled. "Well, it might be the best medicine—something to get your blood going—clear out your passages. I'll write out a prescription of "Do Not Disturb" and put it on the door." He turned and left the room as Rona followed closely behind, locking the door as soon as he was gone. She turned and stripped off her clothing as she made her way slowly, seductively, back to Rock's bed.